Gold Rush Bride Caroline

By Linda Shenton Matchett

St. Joseph, MO
May 15, 1859

Chapter One

"I ought to put a hole in you right now." Finger resting on the trigger, Caroline Vogel squinted through the sight of her rifle. "But I'll give you one more chance to make good."

"This is none of your business," said Willis Baldridge, the swarthy man she'd found whipping the beautiful white horse, who looked like he hadn't bathed in a month. His greasy hair hung to his shoulders under a beat-up hat, and his dirt-encrusted fingernails were ragged. His words whistled between the gaps in his tobacco-stained teeth as he glared at her.

"Wrong answer."

He glowered at the pistol she'd made him toss on the ground near her feet. "Okay. You win, but this isn't over."

"Sure it is." She lowered the weapon, then dug into the pocket of her bloomers and tossed a fistful of coins at the man. "I'll buy your horse. That's double what the mare is worth. And I'll be telling the sheriff about your penchant for abusing animals. Good luck with being able to buy another mount." Her gaze flicked to the cowering squaw behind him. "I imagine you don't treat your woman any better." She sent what she hoped was an encouraging smile at the woman. "You're welcome to join me in the gold fields. I'm getting ready to buy my supplies, and I'd be happy to include enough for you."

Sunlight shimmered on the woman's ebony hair as she shook her head, eyes downcast, hands clasped in front of her. Her moccasin-shod feet shuffled in the dust, her thin shoulders hunched inward. Her beaded dress had seen better days, but the intricacy of the design spoke of creativity and skill.

Caroline sighed. Would the woman pay for her interference? Anger simmered behind the fear in the man's glare. "I'm staying at the Crescent Hotel if you change your mind. Ask for Caroline Vogel. You don't need a man to take care of you, and even if you did, I doubt this *coyote* knows how to treat you properly."

"It's bad enough you're stealing my horse, you ugly witch. You got no right to my woman."

Her stomach clenched, and she resisted the urge to pull up the bandanna that had slipped down, uncovering the scars that crisscrossed her neck. "I *purchased* the horse, and no one has a right to anyone else. She gets to choose whether she wishes to be with you."

"You must be one of those abolitionists. But in this case, you're wrong. Her father traded her fair and square, and she knows that. Now, butt out."

"All right." She gestured with the gun's barrel. "But I don't want to see you again. You should crawl back under the rock from which you slithered."

The man wrapped his fingers around the squaw's upper arm in a viselike grip and yanked her toward him. She flinched, but risked a peek at Caroline from under her bangs. An imperceptible shrug lifted one slender shoulder.

"You better hope I don't see you again," he snarled. "It won't go well for you." He turned on his heel and dragged the woman down the street.

Caroline blew out a deep sigh and fought the urge to race after the pair. She knew little about the ways of the various tribes that populated the land. Was the woman's father truly allowed to barter her like a cow? Unlike many people she knew, she didn't believe the Natives were barbarians, but were their ways so different than the white people that children weren't a gift, but rather chattel with which to bargain?

She uncocked the rifle, settled her bandanna in place, then peered down the street at the signs over the doors. At the end of the block, she spotted a large sign on a barnlike building: Randolph Riggs Animal Doctor. Boots clomping on the hard-packed ground, she led the horse in a steady walk. She raised her hand to knock, then spied a wrought-iron bell, so she tugged on the rope, wincing as the clapper clanged.

Footsteps sounded from deep inside the house, then the door opened to reveal a disheveled man with graying hair and gold-rimmed spectacles. "May I help you?"

She gestured toward the horse. "I recently *liberated* this horse from its owner, and as you can see, the poor thing has had a difficult time of it. I'd appreciate your help in bringing her back to full health."

A deep frown creased his forehead, and he rushed past her to the animal. He stroked the mare's muzzle, then murmured as he examined her injuries. Finished with his examination, he turned to Caroline, his mouth set in a slash. "I'd like to keep her overnight for observation, but I'm optimistic that her physical wounds should heal. Her spirit may take longer to recover, if at all."

"Thank you." She could relate. Swallowing against the lump in her throat, she dipped her head in acknowledgment, then hurried back toward the mercantile. It seemed she'd be able to count on at least one man to be kind. *Of course, the man is a doctor...well, the animal version anyway, so he'd have to be nice. It's the rest of the male population that leaves much to be desired.*

Caroline frowned as her mother's voice intruded into her thoughts. *The many times she'd reminded her of the positive attributes of men. Granted, some are out there, but where?* "Father is a good man, loving and kind, but he treats me with pity, indicating he sees me as less than I could be." Her lips trembled, and she cleared her throat. "That's why I left home. To prove to him and everyone else that I don't need a man to take care of me. I'll be just fine on my own."

Chapter Two

Oliver Llewellyn tugged his brimmed hat lower on his head and pulled his leather coat closer as he dodged another puddle. The skies opened two hours ago as dawn broke, sending sheets of rain onto the slumbering town, but he didn't have the luxury of staying inside to wait out the storm. The wagon train was due to leave on the morrow, and he should have been here three days ago to secure a place as second boss.

First, the train had derailed, then one of the stagecoach horses went lame. If it wasn't for the peace he felt each time he prayed about his decision, he'd think he misread God's leading about him to take his current mission.

Most of his assignments since joining the Pinkerton Agency after the war with the Mexicans were on the East Coast. He'd guarded wealthy businessmen, tracked escaped criminals, foiled two bank robberies, and infiltrated a gang. Life had been anything but boring.

What would this new post bring? Keeping an eye on some rich young lady while she panned for gold shouldn't be too difficult. The worst part would be pretending to be caught up in gold fever. Mr. Pinkerton had explained that the Panic of '57 closed opportunities for young men, so many of them came with the hope of striking it rich. Others were simply looking for adventure. Some were avoiding the increasing tensions between the North and South. Personally, he was glad to be away from the difficult atmosphere.

He strode past the mercantile, several saloons, a couple of restaurants, and the livery. Leaving the main part of town, he spied smoke curling from the chimney above the blacksmith shop. The breeze shifted and sent the acrid fumes in his direction. Admiring the man's wares displayed on the porch, he passed the barnlike building.

Like a fleet of their namesake, dozens of prairie schooners sat in the expansive fields. Men, women, and children crawled in and out of the ungainly wagons preparing for the day. How many of them were gold seekers?

As he approached the bustling campsite, the rain dissipated to a fine mist, and patches of blue appeared among the gray clouds. His feet sank into the sodden ground. He stopped next to a man wrestling with a large canvas sheet. "Help you, sir?"

Deeply tanned with sun-bleached hair, the man gave him a curt nod. "Much obliged."

In moments, they had folded the recalcitrant material and strapped it to the side of the wagon. The man gestured toward the heavens. "With the weather we didn't make no fire, so I can't offer you any coffee, but if you're hungry, we've got hardtack and biscuits."

"I've had my fill already, but thanks for the offer." Oliver surveyed the area. "I'm looking for the trail boss, Micah Urqhart. He around?"

Pivoting on his heel, the man squinted into the distance, then pointed at a large man wearing a white broad-brimmed hat. "That's him. Always wears a white hat so he can be spotted right quick. Seems like an all right fella."

Oliver shook the man's hand. "Thanks, Mr...?"

"Dempsey. Gil Dempsey. Any time." With a wave, Mr. Dempsey climbed into the wagon.

Threading his way through the chaos, Oliver made his way to the far end of the site. He waited until the trail boss finished giving directions to a lanky boy, who appeared to be thirteen or fourteen years of age. Like a puppy, the young man hadn't grown into his limbs and seemed eager to please as he nodded and galloped toward a group of men working with some oxen.

"Mr. Urqhart, my name is Oliver Llewellyn. I wrote to you about being your second and wondered if the job was still available."

A beefy man, the trail boss towered over Oliver's six-foot-four-inch frame and outweighed him by at least a hundred pounds. He turned and lifted an eyebrow. "I expected you days ago. What gives?"

"Transportation problems. First the train, then the stage. We were stuck in between towns or I'd have sent a wire."

Micah frowned. "Confounded trains. Supposedly the wave of the future, but I'm not so sure about that." He pushed his hat off his forehead.

"Job's yours. I haven't seen anyone in this ragtag collection of folks who is qualified. It will be interesting to see if they all make it to their destination. Unfortunately, your gun skills from the war may come in handy. What else can you tell me about yourself?"

"I'm a good tracker. And scavenger. I was a scout for the last half of the conflict."

"Perfect." Micah held out his hand. "Welcome aboard."

Oliver shook his hand, then looked over the trail boss's shoulder at the activities among the wagons. "I'm surprised to see so many women. Families. Are these fortune hunters really going to take young'uns with us?"

"Not all of them are headed for the gold fields. Quite a few of them lost their homes in the Panic. Looking to start fresh in the fertile lands of the West." Micah eyed Oliver. "You ever been in this neck of the woods?"

"Yep. My parents settled in Wisconsin when they first came to America, but they tired of the winters and headed to Kansas territory. They died in the flood of forty-four."

"I'm sorry to hear that. That was a rough time. I heard it rained for six straight weeks."

"You heard correctly. Our cabin was swept down the Mississippi River, along with a bunch of others, but I wasn't home at the time. If I had been—"

Micah squeezed his shoulder. "You might not be here. Can't blame yourself. The Lord called them home, and it's not ours to reason why." He jerked his head toward a wagon parked at the edge of the field. "We've got us a young woman who's traveling on her own. A few other women are traveling in groups, but she's the only one alone. Before we head out tomorrow, I'm gonna make it clear that they'll all be expected to keep up. No special treatment. They've gotta hold their own." He shoved his hands into his pockets. "And if I was a betting man, I'd wager most of them will turn back. However, that one gal seems to have spunk. She's tall for a woman, sturdy, so she's got that going for her. But she comes from money, so I'm not sure how much she's had to do for herself. I'd like you to keep an eye on her the first couple of days. Get a feel for whether she's got what it takes."

"Does she have a name?"

"Caroline Vogel. She spent last night in a hotel. Does that give you an indication of what we might be up against?"

Oliver schooled his features. The trail boss had just assigned him to watch the woman he was being paid to guard.

Chapter Three

Ignoring the stares and scowls at her bloomers, Caroline marched down the sidewalk carrying her satchel in one hand, and her rifle in the other. The mattress at the hotel left much to be desired, but she'd wanted one last night on a real bed. Lying on the ground or inside the wagon to sleep was sure to be hard. It would be a long month of travel. No doubt the men on the journey expected her to complain or find conditions difficult, but she wouldn't give them the satisfaction of seeing her discomfort.

The rain had finally cleared, but the humidity thickened the air, and her curls tried to break free from the pins that bound her hair. She should have braided her red tresses, but her garment was shocking enough. Perhaps when they got on the trail and away from the restraints of society, she could loosen her appearance.

She rolled her eyes. Since when did she give two hoots about what people thought of her? She no longer had to worry about being an embarrassment to her parents. Starting tomorrow, she would dress to meet the demands of the trip, not to abide by the rules of *Godey's Lady's Book* that had no bearing on reality.

Reaching the end of town, she stepped off the wooden planks and onto the saturated ground. Her boots squished as she walked, but at least she wasn't dragging long skirts through the mud. Another reason to wear her unorthodox outfit.

The trail boss hadn't commented about her garment, but he'd studied her for a long while before explaining his expectations for the trip. He'd seemed more concerned about her ability to keep up and do her part than what she wore. The look in his eyes told her he didn't think she'd succeed. He commented about the value of her items and intimated she couldn't look after herself.

She'd prove him wrong.

Conversations and laughter mingled with creaking wagons, bellowing oxen, and clanking metal.

"Miss?" A voice sounded behind her. "Miss!"

Caroline turned.

Bruised and disheveled, the Indian woman from yesterday hurried toward her. "I want to go with you."

"Are you all right?" Caroline's stomach hollowed. "Do you need to see a doctor?"

"No doctor. I will be fine, but I must get away." The woman grimaced. "The wagons leave today, yes?"

"Yes, and, of course, you may accompany me." Caroline's mind raced. She'd purchased more than the required supplies, but would they be sufficient for the two of them?

The woman dug into her leather bag. "I have money. I can pay."

With a dismissive wave, Caroline shook her head. "Save that for another time. I can afford the items, but we may need to return to the mercantile to purchase more. I'll ask the trail boss to wait for us. He won't be happy, but that can't be helped." Warmth spread through her. She'd have a companion for the journey. "You can't keep calling me Miss. My name is Caroline. What is yours?"

"Little Doe. It wouldn't be proper for me to use your name."

"Nonsense. We're going to share a wagon and a campfire. There's no need to stand on formalities."

A smile bloomed on Little Doe's face, and she nodded, tears filling her eyes. "Thank you."

"Does that wastrel of a man know you've left him?"

The young woman's eyes clouded. "He was still...uh...asleep."

"You mean unconscious from too much liquor."

"Yes."

"Is that what happened after we parted ways? He got drunk and took out his anger at me on you?"

Little Doe pressed her lips together.

"We ought to bring charges against the varmint, but I doubt the law would do anything on your behalf. Being a woman and a Native are two strikes, aren't they? Anyway, we'll say no more about this unless you wish to discuss it." Caroline grinned. "Let the adventure commence."

They wended their way through the campsite until they reached Caroline's wagon. She opened the flap on the canvas cover and climbed inside, then gasped. Someone had stolen a portion of her provisions. Who would do such a thing? And why?

Her shoulders sagged for a brief moment, then she straightened her spine. She would not let this discourage her. Perhaps the trail boss already knew about it and planned to tell her when she arrived.

She scrambled to the ground, her mouth set in a firm line. "Remain with the wagon, Little Doe. I need to see Mr. Urqhart."

The young woman leaned against the massive conveyance, but uncertainty danced across her face.

Caroline squeezed her shoulder. "How about if you wait inside? I won't let anything happen to you."

"Tha—"

"And not another thank-you. We're equals. Friends."

Tears shimmered in Little Doe's eyes, and she hoisted herself into the schooner. Rustling sounded, then all was still.

Blowing out a deep breath, Caroline smoothed the overskirt of her bloomers, then searched for the trail boss's white hat. Bobbing among a crowd of men near the oxen, the hat contrasted with the sea of black and brown hats. Heart pounding, she hurried toward the herd. She'd have preferred to discuss her situation alone with the man, but that didn't appear to be an option.

The stench of manure, mud, and animals met her as she approached, and she wrinkled her nose. "Mr. Urqhart, a moment, please." She shouted to be heard over the noise.

Next to him, a tall man with jet-black hair turned toward her. His broad shoulders strained at his flannel shirt that tapered to a narrow waist. Gray eyes, the color of the sea after a storm, pierced her face. Her breath caught. Older than most of the men in the caravan by at least ten years, he dipped his head in acknowledgment, then jabbed the trail boss and jerked his head toward her.

Mr. Urqhart whirled. "You're late. What kept you?"

"I've run into complications. Someone has pilfered items from my wagon, and someone will be joining me, so I need to purchase more items."

His face darkened. "Stolen? Nobody steals under my watch. Are you sure?"

"Positive." She drew herself to her full height, but still had to tilt her neck to look him in the eye. "I don't appreciate you questioning the veracity of my claim. And apparently people do steal under your watch. I will need an hour to return to the store to acquire additional supplies."

"You're bringing an additional person at the last minute?" The good-looking cowboy glared at her. "These journeys take planning and preparation. You can't just change how many folks are in the train."

Caroline narrowed her eyes at the man. "I don't remember asking for your opinion. I'm discussing my situation with the trail *boss,* so you can mind your own business."

"Well, I'm second-in-command, so this is my business." His eyes glittered, darkening to charcoal. "And if you can't be timely or prepared, maybe you're not cut out to be a gold rusher."

Her grip on the rifle tightened, and she stifled the urge to swing it at the man's head. Instead, she counted to ten before speaking. "A valid point, however, I was prepared until your failure to secure the area against thieves."

Mr. Urqhart sputtered, "No one was prowling around your wagon. And no one else complained of loss."

"That you know of. As to the additional member of the party, she will ride in my wagon and partake of my supplies. She is strong and capable, so she can help with tasks along the way."

"Another woman." Mr. Second-in-Command frowned. "We can't be giving you women special treatment."

She lifted her chin. "None is expected. As a former member of the Ponca, Little Doe has more skills in one hand than most people. And having been misused by a drunkard and scalawag, she is in need of a fresh start, so I'll hear no more about her not coming with us. Is that clear?"

The man had the decency to look upset at her declaration, but his stance remained unbending. "Crystal."

"Now, if you *gentlemen* will excuse me, I must return to town."

Before either could reply further, she pivoted and stalked away. How dare they assume she was lying about the missing items. Had they taken them? The trail boss made it clear yesterday he wasn't happy with her and the other single women being part of the train. He'd stopped short of calling them camp followers, but it would be an uphill battle to prove her integrity. With any luck, she and Little Doe could avoid the handsome cowboy with eyes the color of burnished pewter.

Oliver exchanged a glance with Micah. The feisty woman had flustered him more than he wanted to admit. More beautiful in person than the photo he'd been given, she had green eyes that flashed with intelligence, and her creamy complexion made his fingers itch to see if her skin was as soft as it appeared. He couldn't wait to see the sunlight turn her red hair into glistening flames of color. He'd been so tongue-tied, he hadn't given the woman his name. Just made demands. He'd been stunned to learn her wagon mate was a Native but was not surprised she'd been maltreated. He'd seen too many instances of this behavior in his travels. Miss Vogel had a good heart to take in the woman. And instead of barking at her, he should have said as much.

Micah grinned. "She's going to be a handful. I should have warned you. Met her yesterday when she dropped off her wagon. She's no shrinking violet, and she handles that rifle like she was born to it."

"You noticed that." Oliver chuckled. "Maybe you should have made her second-in-command."

"Ha. Not likely." Micah cast an eye at the sky. "Not real happy to be held up by this, but she doesn't strike me as one to tell tall tales. Hopefully, we can make up the time along the way."

Oliver removed his hat and finger combed his hair before slapping the hat back on. "How successful have you been with that in the past?"

A wordless shrug from the boss told him what he already suspected. Leading a procession of waddling wagons was going to be more difficult than herding cats.

Micah gestured to a trio of men arguing about thirty yards away. "The women may be the least of our worries. I'll be back."

"No, let me handle this. They need to get used to me telling them what to do."

"Good point. Have at it."

Squaring his shoulders, Oliver tramped across the damp ground to the three men who looked close to exchanging fisticuffs. "Good morning, fellas. I wanted to introduce myself. I'm Oliver Llewellyn, second to the trail boss. How are things going?"

As if he'd thrown a bucket of water on them, the squabblers separated. The smallest of the men gave him a black look, but the other two offered tentative smiles. Of medium build and wearing a blue flannel shirt, the blond man stuck out his hand. "Glad to meecha. Cody's my name." Pointing to the tall, bearded man to his left, he said, "This is Everett, and the other guy is Levi. We're raring to go."

"Shouldn't be much longer. One of our travelers ran into some difficulties, so we'll leave later than planned. If you're looking to kill some time, I believe Mr. Urqhart could use a hand with the stock."

"Sure, I could do that."

Cody nodded, and the two men wandered toward the temporary corral.

"I got things to do," Levi snarled before stalking off.

Oliver watched the surly man for several minutes. Unless Levi changed his attitude, he would bear watching. Had he been responsible for Miss Vogel's missing provisions? Possibly, but just because a man had a vile temper didn't make him a thief. The man ducked into one of the far wagons, and Oliver turned his attention to the rest of the campsite. He studied each group, trying to ascertain whether he had more potential troublemakers.

Micah was counting on him. Was he up to the task of helping lead a mismatched conglomeration of people across the wilds of the Kansas territory? Time would tell. He continued to wander through the field, periodically stopping to chat with the settlers and gold rushers. All seemed eager to get started, but none seemed particularly upset that the train would commence movement later than anticipated.

Thirty minutes later, he'd met everyone, including Little Doe. He'd rapped gently on the side of Miss Vogel's wagon and announced himself.

The Native woman didn't show herself, instead thanking him through the canvas. Her timid voice was tinged with fear, and his throat ached at her pain. He would add her to his growing prayer list.

As he crossed the expanse toward Micah, movement caught his eye. Miss Vogel had returned. His mission had begun.

Chapter Four

A chill descended as the sun dipped below the horizon, and Caroline pulled her coat closer around her body. The soles of her feet burned from the number of miles she'd traversed next to the wagon. Little Doe seemed none the worse for wear, and the farther they traveled away from St. Joseph, the less timid her demeanor. The young woman still cast glances over her shoulder, but not nearly as often as yesterday.

"Halt!" In the distance, the word floated toward Caroline as travelers passed the order from schooner to schooner stretched nearly three-quarters of a mile.

She huffed out a deep sigh and smiled at Little Doe. "How can I be excited yet bored at the same time?"

The young woman rubbed the back of her neck. "I feel the same. Though beautiful, the landscape is beginning to blur together, even after only one day. Perhaps it will change as we move deeper into the west."

"It will, especially as we approach the mountains. I can't wait to see how Pike's Peak differs from the mountains in Georgia." Caroline led the oxen close to the wagon in front of her, then unhitched the beasts.

"What do you want to do for dinner? I hate to admit it, but I'm too exhausted to build a fire."

"You take care of the animals. If you'll collect some wood, I'll make the fire and rustle up some food. We must take advantage of the timber. Eventually, we will be forced to use buffalo chips to burn."

Caroline wrinkled her nose. "Are those what I think they are?"

Little Doe giggled. "Yes. Dung is dried out to make it flammable. An unpleasant but necessary substitute."

"How clever. While preparing for the journey, I read copious newspapers, but the articles conflicted with each other, and they certainly didn't offer helpful tips like alternative fire materials. How can that be if they're reporting about the same topic?"

"Perhaps they are telling people what they want to hear." Little Doe cocked her head. "Would you have come if you knew the journey would be so difficult?"

"Yes, well...maybe." Caroline crawled into the wagon and retrieved two iron skillets from the top of a crate. She handed them to Little Doe, then jumped to the ground. At least the weather had been pleasant. Like Goldilocks's porridge. Not too hot or cold. "I'll be right back with some wood. Select what you'd like from the supplies."

"I will see to it." Little Doe hoisted herself into the wagon.

Whistling, Caroline sauntered to the trees and picked up felled branches. She soon had an armload of kindling, hurried back to dump the collection near Little Doe, then returned to the woods for more. By the time she got back from her third trip, her friend had a fire burning and was paring vegetables for stew. Caroline's mouth watered as she applied the liniment from the doctor on the horse she'd named Spirit for the animal's gentle but intrepid nature. She then hobbled the horse nearby, stroking her muzzle and murmuring softly.

She sauntered to the campfire and squatted on her haunches. "What may I do to help?"

"Nothing." With quick motions, Little Doe spooned dollops of batter onto the bubbling stew, then plunked the empty bowl on the ground and grinned at Caroline. "However, you may wash the dishes when we're done."

"Deal. I'd much rather clean up than cook any day of the week."

"Then I will cook during our journey, and you will wash."

"Are you sure? Shouldn't we swap off?"

"Not unless you want to. I dislike washing up. I enjoy creating the meals. Using what we have to make something delicious and filling."

Caroline rubbed her stomach. "Perfect, because I love to eat delicious and filling food."

Little Doe chuckled, then ducked her head and poked at the dumpling. "A few more minutes, then we will be ready." She cleared her throat. "Should we discuss the assignment of tasks? I have many skills to offer, but I also want to learn those that I'm unfamiliar with."

"I'd be happy to teach you, but we might want to stick with the ones we know best."

"True. But I want to do my part."

"You already have." Caroline leaned forward to peek into the skillet. "I never was good at making bread or biscuits. Mine always came out tough or chewy."

"The secret is not to work the dough too much." Little Doe picked up a tin plate and ran her fingers around the edge. "In addition to cooking, I can do laundry, and I'm good with a needle. Medicine, too."

"Medicine?" Caroline's head shot up. "We should tell the trail boss. He'll want to know that. We'll share the laundry, and I'll let you be the seamstress. I'm no good at that either. But I'm a good shot and can hunt for fresh meat. We'll have to hope the wagon doesn't break down, but if it does, perhaps we can barter for help with that."

"Enough planning. The food is ready." Little Doe dished a large portion of stew and dumplings onto the plate and handed it to Caroline, then served herself.

Caroline forked some of the fragrant mixture into her mouth and moaned. Flavor exploded on her tongue. "This is incredible." She winked. "You are definitely in charge of our meals."

Little Doe's cheeks pinked. "Thank you, but it is not much."

"Don't underestimate yourself, Little Doe. We women have a bad habit of doing that. You are very talented, but you have value just by being human."

A sheen of tears glimmered in the Native woman's eyes, and she nodded.

Caroline watched the activity as the troop settled in for the night. Children cavorted amid the wagons, burning off excess energy. Conversation ebbed and flowed, punctuated by occasional laughter. The familiar white hat appeared at the far end of the encampment as the trail boss visited each group.

"Good evening, Miss Vogel. Little Doe."

Little Doe gasped and put her hand to her chest.

Caroline's head whipped up toward the voice.

Mr. Second-in-Command stood with his hat in his hands. She'd since learned his name was Oliver Llewellyn. "How did you fare today? Everything all right with you?"

"Yes, why wouldn't it be?" She heard the sting in her voice and winced.

"No reason. Micah and I are checking in with each party."

"Oh. Well, we're fine. Thank you for asking. I'm going to gather more firewood shortly, then we'll be turning in for the night."

"Don't stray too far."

"I know what I'm doing." Caroline's jaw tightened. The man might be handsome, but his arrogance knew no bounds.

"In Georgia, perhaps." His lips twisted. "It is my responsibility to ensure your safe—"

"So this is about you."

"No, I—"

"Little Doe and I appreciate your concern, but we'll be fine." Finished with her meal, she rose and put her hands on her hips. "I'm sure there are others who could use your assistance."

He held his hands up in surrender, backed away from the fire, then turned on his heel, and strode toward the next wagon.

"He means well." Little Doe's voice was soft. "He has kind eyes. I trust him."

Caroline's jaw dropped as she studied her friend. The woman had a right not to trust any man, yet after two days the young woman was comfortable with Oliver. "I'll be back shortly." She headed for the tree line.

"I think you like him, too." Laughter colored Little Doe's voice.

"Hardly." Caroline stomped into the forest and bent to pick up a branch. Rough hands grabbed her from behind, and she squealed. A dirty palm clamped over her mouth. Struggling to get away, she bit one of the calloused fingers, and her assailant grunted and slapped her. Ears ringing, she wiggled in his arms and swung her leg in an attempt to kick the man, whose fetid breath brushed her cheek. Dinner roiled in her stomach. She stomped her heel onto the top of his foot.

He howled, then rasped, "You got guts. I'll give you that."

Her attacker was Little Doe's abuser. She shuddered. He'd apparently tracked them to the wagon train, then followed the caravan and waited for a chance to catch her alone. Her blood boiled. She was not going to let him get the best of her. She jabbed her elbows and stomped her feet, pummeling him as much as she could.

With a yelp, he fell away from her in a heap.

Fists clenched, and breath heaving, she whirled.

Oliver stood over the man, a Colt revolver pointed at his quivering form. "Get up, and don't make any sudden motions. I've got an itchy trigger finger."

The man glared at Oliver, but did as he was told.

"Now, we're going to head back to camp where the trail boss will decide what happens to you. If you're lucky, he won't hang you."

"Hang me! I haven't—"

"Because you didn't get a chance. But attacking a woman is a serious offense." Oliver glanced at her. "Are you okay?" His smoky-gray eyes were nearly black in the inky darkness, but she felt his probing look.

"Yes." Her pulse skittered.

"Good. Please follow us so you can report exactly what happened. Micah will want to know." He poked her aggressor. "Get moving."

Looking mulish, the man held up his arms and headed toward the camp.

Caroline trailed behind them, her body trembling. With shaking hands, she wrapped her bandanna in place around her neck. Had Oliver seen her scars? The disgust on his face seemed to have been directed at her attacker, but time would tell. *Thank You, Lord, for sending Oliver to help, but did You do that on purpose? You know I don't like to be beholden to a man.*

Chapter Five

As they approached the camp, Oliver caught sight of Micah and whistled, a long, piercing blast followed by three short ones. The trail boss whirled and ran toward them, a dark frown etched on his face.

Oliver gestured with his gun. "This scoundrel attacked Miss Vogel. Was going to abduct her."

Micah's frown deepened, and he pulled his pistol from the holster. "I'll take him." His gaze flicked to Miss Vogel. "Did he harm you in *any* way?"

"No." Her face warmed. "Mr. Llwellyn stopped him."

"She gave almost as good as she got, Micah. But someone should look at her."

"Little Doe has healing skills." She wrapped her arms around her middle. "If it's all the same to you, I'd like to return to my wagon. I know I should give you my report, but—"

"Tomorrow is soon enough, Miss Vogel. I'm glad you're okay." Micah prodded her assailant. "Get going. I've got just the place for you."

As the pair marched toward camp, Caroline's shoulders sagged, and she nodded, then turned to Oliver. "Is this where you give me a lecture and an 'I told you so'?"

"Tempting, but no." He shrugged. It was his fault the attack occurred. He should have been more vigilant. He had one job: to keep the young woman from harm, and he'd blown it. "Even I didn't figure on a two-legged animal. But I will say, it's best for you to have your gun with you at all times."

"Agreed." She lifted her chin. "I won't be caught by surprise again."

He crooked his arm and sent her a teasing grin. "Not that you need help, but let me escort you to your wagon."

A giggle escaped, and her cheeks pinked, bringing color back to her ashen face. "I accept, kind sir." She tucked her hand in the bend of his elbow.

Her warmth permeated his coat sleeve. Or was he imagining things? Despite her height, he still had to dip his head to meet her eyes. Perspiration sprang out on his forehead. He needed to remain aloof. He cleared his throat as the sauntered across the grassy expanse. "How many others did you anger while in St. Joseph? Could there be anyone tracking you from Georgia?"

"What? No!" She yanked her hand away. "And he had no right treating his horse or Little Doe like he did."

He tucked her fingers through the crook of his arm, then laid his hand on top of them. "Of course he didn't, but I need to understand what we're dealing with. The safety of this group is my priority, and if there are bad men headed this way, Micah and I have to be prepared."

She blew out a loud sigh. "You're right. I'm sorry to be defensive. I'm not aware of anyone else who would be searching for me." She licked her lips. "And I appreciate what you did to...uh...rescue me."

"You did most of the work. Like I said to Micah, you gave him a run for his money. If you'd have had your weapon, he wouldn't have stood a chance." He chuckled. "Bet he's not the first man to underestimate you."

Her flush told him he was right.

"Did your dad teach you to shoot?"

"Yes, but my mom could have. She's a crack shot."

His eyebrows lifted. "So you come from a family of gunslingers."

"Hardly. Mom learned in the gold fields. She and her first husband did real well, and he was often gone, taking their findings to the bank."

"She sounds like quite a woman."

Miss Vogel's lips twisted. "She is, although she tried to talk me out of coming on this trip. I don't understand why. She had her adventure. Why can't I have mine?"

"I don't know this for sure, but I would imagine when one becomes a parent, adventure holds less allure." He patted her hand.

"Listen, after all this, can you call me Oliver? Formality seems rather contrived out here."

"I'd like that." Her teeth flashed in the moonlight as she smiled. "And you may call me Caroline."

"A pretty name." His pulse quivered. So much for remaining detached. "You did a good job back there. I could teach you some specific moves that I learned in my military training. Even without a gun, you'd be able to fend off an assailant."

"I'd like that, but we should teach all the women."

"A good idea." Disappointment clawed him. "Will you help me convince them?"

"It might take a bit." Her eyes narrowed. "But you'll need to persuade their husbands or fathers. Most men don't want their women to be able to take care of themselves. They want a pretty wife, who will have lots of babies and keep a clean house."

"Personal experience?" He cocked his head at her. "Not all men are shallow or overbearing. And any man who fails to see your beauty is a fool."

"Then Dahlonega was full of fools." She pressed her lips together and ducked her head.

"And more's the pity." He slowed his steps. He was loathe to arrive at her wagon too soon. "No matter what anyone has told you, your scars don't detract from your appearance."

"You haven't seen them in the light of day." Tears glistened in her eyes. "The looks of revulsion tell me differently."

His stomach hollowed at the pain in her voice. She was wounded. Deeply. *Dear God, please heal her. Help her discover her worth and beauty from You.* "It's hard to accept why God allows bad things to happen, isn't it? War, the man who mistreated Little Doe, and the attack that left you scarred are terrible things."

Her eyes widened, and her free hand fluttered to the scarf at her throat. "Yes!"

"And you feel guilty for railing at our heavenly Father about them."

Her face lit up. "You understand."

"Yes. I argued with Him a lot during the war. But he used the experience to shape me. Mold me into the man I am today. And I think He did the same with you. Not many would risk the anger of an other's abuser or take in an Indian woman. Your kindness and acceptance of Little Doe are evidence of your gentle soul." He winked. "Now, if you'll give us guys a chance to prove we're not all idiots."

She snorted a laugh, then covered her mouth for a brief moment, her eyes dancing. "I can't make any promises."

"I have my work cut out for me." A chuckle rumbled in his chest, and he gestured toward the ghostly hulk of her wagon. "Sleep well, Caroline. Rest assured you are safe."

The flap opened from the inside, but Little Doe didn't appear. He'd have to prove his worth to her, too.

"Good night." Caroline crawled into the wagon. "Thank you...Oliver." Low and honey smooth, her use of his name sent his pulse racing.

He scrubbed at his face with cold hands. Two days with this woman, and his world had turned upside down.

Chapter Six

Flames crackled, and Caroline scooted closer to the fire. Warmth spread through her limbs. The days were pleasantly warm, but as soon as the sun slipped below the horizon, temperatures plummeted. The guidebook she'd purchased made a passing mention of the weather, yet here on the trail the elements meant the difference between a good day of travel and a difficult one with little progress. Perhaps when all was said and done, she'd write her own manual.

Fortunately, today was a success. The group had managed to tuck more than twenty miles under its belt. None of the wagons had broken, and the dust was minimal. Everyone seemed to be in a celebratory mood.

Little Doe stood and dipped her head, the blaze reflecting on her bronze skin. She reached for Caroline's plate. "I'll wash the dishes before I go to bed."

Caroline shook her head. "No, you cooked. I can clean up." She grinned. "Or Oliver can take a turn. He's shared dinner every night this week."

He chuckled. "Absolutely. You worked enough for one day, Little Doe. And it's been my pleasure to dine with you ladies."

The Native woman ducked her head as pink tinged her cheeks. "Thank you Mr. Llwellyn."

"Oliver. I told you to call me Oliver."

"Oliver." Little Doe climbed into the wagon and tied the canvas flap. Rustling sounded for a few moments, then all was quiet.

"She seems to be more at ease with you." Caroline poked one of the logs, and sparks shot into the air. "Thank you for being so kind to her. Not all our fellow travelers are happy she's part of the troop."

"Has anyone been especially rude?"

"No. She stays close to the wagon, and most folks ignore her. Some give her ugly looks, but few have the confidence to address her outright."

"Not with you by her side carrying a gun." One corner of his lip lifted in a crooked smile. "They're wise to keep their distance."

A giggle slipped out, and Caroline rubbed her hands together. "I wouldn't shoot them."

"Why take the chance?" He tossed his plate on the ground and leaned back on his elbows, stretching out his long legs. The orange glow from the fire created angles and planes on his rugged face. His pewter-colored eyes glinted.

Caroline licked her dry lips. She'd wanted to prove she could take care of Little Doe and herself, but the incident with her assailant still weighed heavily. Unfamiliar noises made her heart race, and the hair on the back of her neck often prickled. Bravado was foolish and could get a person killed. Having Oliver share their fire ensured their safety, and whether she wanted to admit it or not, she'd grown to enjoy his company.

Clever and well-spoken, he regaled them with stories, many of which poked fun at himself. During the days, he rode up and down the line of wagons ensuring everyone was safe and moving. Little Doe claimed he tarried with them longer than he did with the others. He treated Caroline with respect, often asking her opinion on a matter or seeking her thoughts about a traveler. He was simply doing his job. Wasn't he?

She peeked at him from under her bangs and caught him staring. Her pulse skittered, but she refused to break eye contact. She cocked her head. "Something you want to say?"

"I hate to ruin the pleasant atmosphere, but you need to know we'll be heading into Arapaho territory in the next couple of days. Micah will make the announcement tomorrow morning as we pack up to get moving. Everyone will need to be extra vigilant." He picked up a small log and tossed it onto the blaze. "It will be best if Little Doe remains inside the wagon as much as possible."

"You think if the Indians spot her, they'll make trouble for us?"

"They might think she's a captive."

"But what if they're her people? Should we ask what she wants to do? She might wish to return to them."

"Possibly. We'll talk to her, but nearly all the tribes are nomadic. She may not know where to find her family. The Act that forced them to move changed their migration patterns. They—" He lifted his head and surveyed the area. His gaze ricocheted from wagon to wagon.

A chill slithered up her spine. "What is it?"

"Maybe nothing." His lips barely moved as he spoke, his voice pitched low. "But I get the distinct impression we're being watched."

Her skin crawled, and she fought the urge to dive into the wagon.

"What should we do?"

Oliver had to give Caroline credit. She put on a brave face, but her voice wavered. He continued to probe the darkness with his eyes. "I'll talk to Micah about posting more guards."

"I can take a shift."

He shook his head. "It's more important that you stay close to Little Doe."

Even in the firelight, her face paled, but she straightened her spine and gave him a curt nod. "I can do that. Should we tell Little Doe of our concerns?"

"Yes, she should be prepared." Oliver climbed to his feet, letting his arms dangle in an attempt to appear casual. He cast a quick scan around the campsite. It appeared everyone had retired for the night. Even Micah's white-hatted head was not in sight. Was no one else concerned? Perhaps he was worrying for nothing.

Caroline rose, grabbed the lantern, and went to the wagon. She untied the flap and crawled inside, then held the canvas open so he could follow her.

He folded his lanky frame into the crowded space.

Little Doe bolted upright and shrank against the canvas wall. Her eyes widened, and her jaw dropped. "M-Mr. Llewellyn?"

With hands raised in surrender, he sent her what he hoped was an encouraging smile. "I'm not here to stay, Little Doe. We may have...uh...a situation."

She wrapped her arms around her middle, and her lower lip trembled. "Willis Baldridge?"

Oliver lowered his arms. "No. He's gone. Two of the men agreed to take him back to St. Joseph. They'll drop him off with the sheriff, then return. Without wagons, they'll be able to make good time and catch up to us." He took a deep breath. "I've no proof at this point, but I believe we're being watched. An announcement is going to be made tomorrow that we're headed into Arapaho territory within the next couple of days, but we're close enough that the tribe could have scouts keeping an eye on us."

"How long?"

He exchanged a glance with Caroline, then looked at Little Doe. "Most of today. As I said, nothing definitive, but after two years in a war zone, I've learned to trust my gut. It's telling me we've got some possibly non-friendlies in the area."

"And if they see me, they'll think I'm your prisoner. They may try to rescue me and kill the others in the train during their raid."

"Yes. I'd like you to stay near the wagon, inside as much as possible."

"I could disguise myself as a white woman."

"You would be willing to do tha—" He put a finger to his lips. A nicker sounded outside, then the soft clop of horse hooves. Spirit and his own mount were hobbled several yards away. If he wasn't mistaken, his fears had just materialized outside the wagon. He pointed to both women. "Wait here, until I call for you."

They nodded in unison, then Caroline handed him the lantern.

He poked his head out the flap, and his stomach lurched. Five braves clustered around the back of the vehicle. On the one hand, their low number, and the fact none pointed a weapon at him seemed to indicate a desire to talk. On the other, the young men might be a decoy to lull them into a false sense of security. A larger band might be waiting among the trees.

With a smile, he hopped out of the wagon. "Greetings. What brings you to visit our camp?"

"You approach our lands. State your business."

Oliver lifted one eyebrow. The young man's command of English, though stilted, was good. "We're a mixed group. Many of us are headed to Pike's Peak to seek gold. The rest will be continuing on to Oregon Territory."

"How many?"

His military training made him loathe to give the man information, but if he'd been watching, he probably already knew. "There are about one hundred in our party, six of those are women and fifteen children."

The brave studied him for a long moment. "One of those women is Ponca. Not tied up. Why?"

"She chose to accompany us."

"Accompany?" The man's brow wrinkled.

"Come with us." Oliver nodded. "Would you like to speak with her?"

Turning, he conferred with the others.

Heart thundering in his chest, Oliver tried to read their faces, but their expressions were impassive. If he were a poker player, he wouldn't bet against them.

After several minutes, one of the braves drew his bow and pulled an arrow from the animal-hide quiver on his back, but he didn't nock the shaft. Their spokesman nodded. "Bring her out."

Oliver's mouth dried. Did the man plan to kill the young squaw or him? Or both? *Dear God, keep us safe.*

Chapter Seven

Palms slick with perspiration, Caroline stood between Little Doe and Oliver. Little Doe's posture was straight and proud, like nothing Caroline had seen since meeting the young woman. Oliver's form was taut, like the string on the brave's bow. His hand dangled below his holster, but she had no doubt he could draw with speed and accuracy. The air crackled with tension.

Dinner sat in her stomach like a stone, Little Doe's delicious meal now bitter and sour. While the braves talked among themselves, movement caught her vision from the corner of her eye. She slid her gaze toward the action.

The man in the next wagon popped his face out between the canvas flap, then disappeared back inside. The same thing happened in several vehicles. Would the travelers hide from perceived danger or rush to their aid, guns blazing?

Oliver gave her an imperceptible nod, then rolled his eyes toward the far end of the encampment where Micah's white hat broke the darkness. He strode toward them, hand raised in greeting. Word had obviously reached the trail boss of the Natives' appearance. Or perhaps he'd seen them during his constant vigilance.

"I'm Micah Urqhart, head of this wagon train. Something we can do for you?"

The speaker for the braves gestured to Little Doe. "This woman. We want to know if she's prisoner."

"Absolutely not. Everyone in this party is here because they want to be." He smiled at the young woman. "And she's been an important part of the group, helping with chores and taking care of our injuries and illnesses. She's a healer."

Little Doe nodded and said something in her language. They conversed for two or three minutes until the young woman turned toward Micah and said, "Lone Wolf is willing to let us pass. He believes my story, that I'm not your captive. He will spread the word that we are to pass through their territory safely."

Relief smoothed the lines from Micah's face. "Well, that's good news." He smiled at Lone Wolf. "Much obliged."

Oliver nodded, but his stance remained stiff. Caroline pressed a hand against her racing heart. Did he see something in the Indian that concerned him?

"No hunting." Lone Wolf gestured to the brave on his left, and the young man put away the bow and arrow. "Too many white men are killing the buffalo."

"Fair enough." Micah pushed his hat off his forehead. "Can you show me your boundaries?"

"Boundaries?"

"Where your property starts and ends."

"I can draw in the dust."

Micah pointed to his wagon across the field. "I've got a pencil and paper."

"Of course." Lone Wolf made a motion with his hand, and his companions wheeled their horses and melted into the trees. He dismounted, dipped his head toward Little Doe, and followed Micah.

Caroline blew out a deep breath and sagged against Little Doe. Perhaps Mother and Father were right. Women had no place striking out on their own. She'd never admit it to Oliver, but she was glad he'd been nearby when the braves arrived. Micah, too. "That was a close one."

"Their tribe has already lost too many men. They don't want any trouble."

"Are you sure of that?" Oliver narrowed his eyes. "They could be leading us into a trap."

Little Doe shook her head. "I don't think so." She shuddered. "After being with Willis, I can read the signs of deceit. Lone Wolf is telling the truth."

He shrugged. "Maybe. I've heard too many stories about Indians claiming to be friendly, then turning up later to massacre the whole lot. They hate us and have every right to, but I'm not going to let them catch us by surprise. We're going to double the guard tonight." He touched the brim of his hat and stalked away.

Caroline tugged at her collar. "I don't know about you, Little Doe, but sleep isn't going to be easy."

Little Doe's forehead creased. "They meant what they said. If they wanted to kill us, we'd already be dead." She climbed into the wagon and beckoned Caroline to join her.

With a last look at Oliver's retreating figure, she hoisted herself under the canvas, then slid under the covers. Moments later, Little Doe's breathing was deep and even, but Caroline's mind played the event over and over. Was Little Doe right that the Natives wanted no trouble? Or was Oliver right, and the travelers could expect an attack at some point?

An owl hooted in the distance, followed by an answering call nearby. Like the gonging of a bell, the two birds called back and forth. Back and forth. Caroline sighed and plucked at the blanket that did nothing to soften the wood of the wagon bed.

Footsteps approached, and she smiled into the darkness. She'd recognize Oliver's tread anywhere. A shadow passed, then hovered at the end of the vehicle. Was he going to stand sentry on her doorstep all night? Her skin warmed at his proximity. Sleep wouldn't be coming anytime soon.

The chilly night breeze brushed Oliver's cheeks like a caress. He strained his ears toward the canvas that sheltered Little Doe and Caroline. Silence. Then shuffling. More silence. More shuffling. A sigh. Sleep was proving to be elusive to at least one of the wagon's occupants, and if he were a betting man, he'd say it was Caroline.

He'd experienced the same sort of restlessness on more than a few occasions. The feeling like his blood was surging through his veins and his brain was on fire.

She had to have been frightened, but she held her own during the interaction with the braves. Her protectiveness of Little Doe probably outweighed her fear. He'd have liked to have been there when she'd taken on the squaw's captor. Watching her carve the man down in size with her acerbic tongue and steady aim with a gun.

No wonder the man had been angry. Bested by a woman. A stunning, statuesque woman.

Whoa. Where did that thought come from? He blinked and shook his head. He'd met other beautiful women in his past. Why did this one affect him as she did?

He stuffed his hands in his pockets and paced. Who was he kidding? He knew exactly what drew him to her, and it wasn't only her external appearance. She wasn't like anyone he'd ever met. Her wit was razor sharp, and her intellect just as keen. Their conversations over dinner had been rousing discussions about a wide variety of topics from politics to society's traditions. She hadn't shied away from conflict, often seeming to play devil's advocate just to see what he'd say.

Well-read, she also liked to talk about books she'd read, some of which he'd never heard of. Her parents had raised her to keep current with the news, so she was versed in the latest headlines, including the growing tensions between the North and South, which would eventually escalate to armed conflict unless one side backed down. One war was enough for him.

More sighs filtered out of the wagon, Caroline's frustration at her insomnia evident. If he had the nerve, he'd poke his head in and invite her to keep him company. Which would totally distract him from guard duty.

Good grief. She addled his brain. In the past, he'd have never considered inviting a woman anywhere, let alone to stand guard. He smirked. Although her rifle skills put some of his platoon mates to shame.

She would make some lucky man an excellent wife. Why did that thought hollow his stomach? He wasn't in the market for a mate. Ever. His job with Pinkerton precluded him from marrying and having children. Sure, lots of the agents had families, but some of them died in the field, and that wasn't fair to those left behind.

No, he could never wed, no matter how tempting the prospect.

Chapter Eight

Stars twinkled in the blackness overhead. Oliver snuck a glance across the fire at Caroline. The flames created a rosy glow on her cheeks, and sparkled in her eyes. Silence blanketed the camp with the occasional snort or whinny from one of the animals.

Two weeks had passed since their encounter with the Indians, and they'd been true to their word. The wagon train had safely traversed the territory and would arrive in Boulder City late tomorrow. As promised, the travelers had refrained from hunting, instead relying on their stores for nourishment. There had been some grumbling, but everyone adhered to the requirement. Even the difficult man from the beginning of the trip.

Little Doe was finally comfortable around him, gently teasing or plying him with food. Her eyes had lost their haunted appearance, and she walked with ease, rather than hunching into herself or disappearing into the wagon as she had when they first met. Faces alight, she and Caroline had discussed their plans for staking their claim. He'd heard Caroline admit that she wasn't looking forward to living in a tent for the foreseeable future, but agreed that taking time to erect a cabin wasn't practical.

If constructing their living quarters wouldn't ruin his cover, he'd have offered to build them. But he was supposed to be as gold hungry as they were. Her parents arranged for his claim to adjoin theirs. Money really could buy anything.

"A nugget for your thoughts."

He chuckled and finger combed his hair. "Just contemplating what the next few days hold. You?"

"Same. I appreciate all you've done for Little Doe and me. Your presence has made the journey easier." She grinned. "But if you ever meet my parents, you can't tell them I said that."

His breath hitched. Hopefully, that would never happen. "Deal." He forced a smile, then gestured to the sky. "How familiar are you with the constellations?"

She craned her neck, her gaze scanning the pinpoints of light. "They all look the same to me. A mishmash of stars."

"Well, if you're going to live in the wilderness, you should learn."

"Dahlonega wasn't exactly a metropolis." She cocked her head. "Especially after the gold played out, and most everyone left for California."

He rose, then circled the fire, and hunkered on the ground next to her. "I'll give you that one. But the stars can act as your guide."

"Did you learn to read the sky during the war?"

"No. My father was fascinated by the heavens. Something he'd learned from his father. Many a night we would sit on the porch and watch the stars appear. He'd share myths and legends about each constellation."

"You were close." She squeezed his hand. "I'm sorry you lost him."

Tingles shot to his elbow, and he swallowed. So much for his vow not to let her affect him. He cleared his throat. "Thank you. I'll see him again one day, but I do miss him. His wisdom. He didn't have a lot of education, but he knew more about life than anyone I've ever met."

"Tell me one of his stories."

"Really?"

"Yes." She nodded and leaned back on her elbows. "Give me a primer on the stars."

"Okay." He reclined, then pointed straight up. "First look for Polaris, the brightest star in the sky. Do you see it?"

She scooted close and aligned her sight with his arm, and the crisp fragrance of soap mingled with lavender wafted past his nose. How did she keep herself fresh and clean-smelling on a six-hundred-mile journey? He blinked and forced his attention back to the sky.

"Yes, there it is. Now, what?"

"Look below it for five stars that resemble the letter W. That is Cassiopeia. Cepheus is to the right of Polaris and is kind of like a stick house."

"I see them!" Caroline squealed and clapped her hands. "Who are they?"

His breath caught, and he had to force himself to watch the sky rather than her exquisite profile. He cleared his throat. "Long ago, in the ancient kingdom of Ethiopia, there lived a king and a queen, Cepheus and Cassiopeia. They had a beautiful daughter named Andromeda. The queen was very vain and boastful, and always getting into trouble. One day, she boasted that her daughter, Andromeda, was more beautiful than all of the daughters of the Sea God, Poseidon. That made Poseidon angry, so he sent a sea monster to attack the king's country. The monster defeated the navy, sank his ships, and destroyed his port cities. Not knowing what else to do, the king appealed to the oracle of the gods for help. Their answer was that he must sacrifice his own daughter, Princess Andromeda, to the sea monster. Dismayed, the king agreed and chained her to the rocks on a cliff to await the monster."

"Oh, no." Caroline frowned. "That's terrible."

He grinned. "You know it's just a story, right? Anyway, the hero Perseus arrived on Pegasus, the winged horse. Perseus took one look at Andromeda, and fell in love. He flew over to the king and queen and asked that he be allowed to marry Andromeda. They agreed, but only if Perseus could save Andromeda and the kingdom from the sea monster. When the monster appeared, Perseus swooped down on it with his sword, and began fighting it. But he was only able to kill the monster by pulling the head of Medusa out from the bag he'd been carrying, and turning

Cetus to stone. So everyone was saved. And they all lived happily ever after.

"What a wonderful story. A bit scary for a child though. Don't you think?"

Oliver shrugged. "For me it was about the adventure."

She sighed and sat up. "My folks meant well when I was growing up, but after the...uh...accident, they treated me with kid gloves. Before then, they'd allowed me to be a tomboy, but afterward, it seemed as if someone was always shadowing me. Keeping watch. I began to feel stifled."

"Did they treat your sister the same?"

"Hardly, but they didn't have to." Her lips twisted. "Abigail is a homebody. She is content to remain indoors reading, doing needlework, or some other girlish activity."

"I would imagine your recovery was long. They feared losing you."

"Yes." She wrapped her arms around her middle. "But I lived. I hate that the attack changed how others saw me."

"Your bandanna. People weren't kind, were they?"

Caroline pressed her lips together and shrugged.

"I hope you eventually believe that scars included, you are a beautiful woman, and anyone who can't see that is an idiot."

She ducked her head, her faced reddening. "You're just being nice, but thank you."

"No, I'm not." He raised one eyebrow. His stomach clenched. He'd never understand the need for some people to wound others with their words. "In the month we've been traveling, have you seen me say something *just to be nice.*"

"Hmm." She tapped her index finger on her chin. "I guess not. But that doesn't mean you can't start. Perhaps the thought of all that gold has scrambled your brain."

He coughed. His brain was muddled, but the condition had nothing to do with lumps of glittering metal. "Everyone has scars, Caroline, not all of them visible." He rubbed at a spot on his pants. "I'm saved by the grace of God, but my past continues to claw at me, leaving unseen cuts."

"You seem so self-assured."

"As do you." He clenched his hands. "But appearances can be deceiving. Life was hard for me after my folks died, and instead of allowing God to help me, I turned my back on Him and made bad choices. Stole to keep myself fed rather than finding a job. Ended up in jail on more than a few occasions."

She laid her hand on his fists. "You were young."

His skin heated, and he laced his fingers with hers. He could get used to cradling her hands in his. "No excuse. I'd been raised right. I was angry that He'd let my parents die, rather than save them. My behavior was pure rebellion. Then I stole from a man who changed my life." He smiled as Enoch's face floated into his mind. "Enoch Snowden was an officer in the army, and rather than charging me with a crime, he took me under his wing. He was a believer, and little by little he reminded me that God loved me, and that even though I didn't understand why He'd let my parents perish in the flood, He was a good and just God. He had my bests interests at heart. I enlisted under his command, and we served in the war together."

"Your voice. I hear regret."

"He was killed at the Battle of Molino del Rey. I never told him how much he meant to me."

"I'm sure he knew." She nudged his shoulder. "And now you're chasing your fortune. What would he think about that?"

Oliver nibbled the inside of his cheek. How to respond? Falsehoods and misdirection were necessary yet evil parts of undercover work. The part he hated. Did God hate it, too? Did the ends justify the means?

"Oliver?"

"Sorry." He extricated his hand and reached for a log. He tossed it onto the fire, sending sparks into the air. He pinned on a smile. "He'd tell me I was a blamed fool, and he'd be right."

She giggled. "Well, we can be fools together."

His stomach roiled. If only she knew the truth.

Chapter Nine

Caroline pulled Spirit to a stop at the edge of Boulder City. She patted the horse's neck and gazed at the teeming street in front of her. Tall men. Short men. Swarthy men. Skinny men. Most unkempt and filthy. The rest only slightly less so.

Seated behind her on the mare, Little Doe gasped.

Restaurants, banks, a laundry, lawyers, and shops lined the wide, dusty road. Caroline's gaze raked in the chaos. To her left, a mercantile stood between a bank and a saloon, both of which had men streaming in and out. Well, they actually staggered from the tavern. Did the men not have claims to work on this gorgeous sunny day?

She glanced at Oliver. "Boulder City is bigger than I imagined. The go-backers we passed over the last few days had me convinced there was nothing here."

"They're the ones who thought the gold was lying on the ground waiting to be picked up and taken to the assayer's office." He shrugged. "Some of the newspaper reports glossed over the amount of work required."

"Were they truly that naïve?"

"Or lazy."

"Hey, good looking," a shrill female voice called from above. "We can give you a warm welcome."

Looking up, Caroline gaped, unable to tear away her gaze.

A voluptuous brunette and a slender blonde hung over the railing waving and winking at Oliver. Their faces were heavily made up, and their hair was swept into elaborate styles. But it was their clothing, or lack thereof, that struck her. Ruffled, knee-length fuchsia skirts barely covered black-lace petticoats, and their boots were adorned with tassels of all things. Sequins glinting in the sunlight, low-cut, off-the-shoulder bodices that left little to the imagination.

"No, thank you, ladies."

Caroline gulped. Her mother had warned her about the soiled doves, but she hadn't expected to see them in broad daylight or on her first foray into town. Her cheeks blazed, and she couldn't bring herself to look at Oliver who'd so casually responded to their lewd invitation.

Did they proposition all men, even those in the presence of another woman? Or did they sense Oliver was unattached?

She'd been about two miles outside of the camp when Oliver had caught up with them. If she didn't know better, she'd think he was following her, but when she quizzed him, he insisted he also needed to record his claim and his presence was coincidence.

He'd done nothing to raise her suspicions on the journey, but his eyes were guarded when he spoke as if some secret lurked. After seeing the chaos and sheer volume of men on the streets, she was glad she hadn't convinced him to ride on ahead of her, no matter what he was hiding. Despite being anxious to get started, she wanted to savor each moment of the adventure, so she'd held Spirit to a walk, drinking in the jagged snowcapped mountains and forested valleys.

"Time's wasting." She blew out a sigh and kneed the horse into a trot.

Oliver's mount kept pace, and they continued through town, slowing when they caught up to an ornate carriage. He jerked his head toward the vehicle. "I'm not sure that's what I'd spend my gold on."

She giggled. "It is a bit much." She read the signs above the buildings. "Which way to the assayer's office?"

He pointed down the street to a line of forty to fifty men snaking from a nondescript doorway. "I believe that's where we're headed."

Her shoulders sagged. "So many of them."

"The office doesn't close for several hours. Let's grab a bite to eat, then come back."

"Are you sure we'll have time?" She nibbled her lower lip. To have come so far only to have to wait was disappointing. "I could stand in line, and you could get the food and bring it back."

"I don't think they'd take too kindly to my cutting in. We should be fine."

Her stomach rumbled, and she pressed a hand against her middle. "Apparently, I'm hungrier than I thought."

Oliver chuckled. "Hold on while I find out what this fine town has to offer in the way of food."

Caroline watched as he guided the horse to the side of the carriage and knocked on the glass. The window slid down, and he doffed his hat as he spoke to the occupant. Even from this distance, she could see the sparkle in his eyes as he conversed. He threw back his head and laughed, creating deep dimples on either side of his mouth. He clapped his hat on his head, covering his blue-black hair from view, then looked toward her and winked.

Her pulse quickened, and her cheeks warmed. Why did she have to blush at the slightest provocation?

He trotted toward them and jerked a thumb over his shoulder. "The gentleman insists the best cook around works at The Surf and Turf. Follow me." He wheeled Ranger and led them to the end of the block, where he dismounted and tied up the horse.

Little Doe slipped to the ground, and Caroline struggled to get down without exposing her entire leg. She'd exchanged her usual bloomers for a traditional dress, a decision she now regretted. She finally gave up and swung down in a swirl of skirts. Smoothing the material, she lifted her chin to find Oliver watching her with amusement. She rolled her eyes and grinned to hide her embarrassment.

They entered the restaurant, and conversation died. A chill swept over Caroline as she surveyed the angry expressions. A clean-shaven man wearing a charcoal-colored suit and crisply ironed white shirt rushed toward them. His eyebrows met in the middle of his forehead, and his mouth was set in a thin line. "You can't come in here."

Next to her, Oliver drew himself to his full towering height, his face a deep red. "Our money is good."

The man shook his head. "I don't doubt it, but *hers* isn't." His eyes slid toward Little Doe. "We don't serve her kind."

Caroline clenched her fists. "How dare you speak about Little Doe like that. Who do you think you are?"

"The owner, and I decide who eats here and who does not. You are welcome to stay." His lip curled. "But your *friend* must wait outside."

"I wouldn't—"

Oliver laid his hand on her arm. "Ladies, we were obviously misinformed about the quality of this establishment." He turned and held the door.

Caroline whirled and marched outside, her blood boiling. Another minute with the man, and she'd have slapped him for his condescending attitude. Little Doe and Oliver followed her onto the wooden sidewalk, his dark eyes like flint.

He bowed to Little Doe. "I apologize for your treatment, Little Doe. The man is a cad and a boor."

The young woman's eyes shimmered with tears. "I don't know why I thought it would be different out here. I'll wait by the horses."

"Nonsense. We're in this together, but we must be practical, so it appears we'll be having a picnic today. You two find a lovely spot where we can dine, and I'll join you shortly." His gaze caressed Caroline's face. "I'm proud of the way you stuck up for Little Doe in there. She's lucky to have you as a friend."

A glow warmed his belly.

Caroline's eyes sparkled at his words, and Oliver's chest swelled. He was glad he could make her feel good about herself. She was a kind and generous woman, and the owner was lucky she hadn't been carrying her rifle. Not that Oliver thought she'd actually shoot the man, but knocking him off his high horse with a little fear wasn't a bad thing.

Oliver touched his fingers to the brim of his hat and pivoted. They'd think him a ninny if he didn't get a move on. He gave himself a mental slap at his failure to realize Little Doe would be refused service. Had he really been foolish enough to think the three of them could sashay into the restaurant like they were gentry? When he returned with the food he'd apologize for his stupidity, and hopefully the young woman wouldn't hold a grudge.

He ducked into the nearest café and strode to the counter. "I need three meals to go," he barked. "What have you got that travels well?"

The freckle-faced young man behind the counter stepped back, his eyes wide. "Uh, fried chicken and all the fixings, sir. Will that be acceptable?"

"I'm sorry. I was a bit forceful, wasn't I?" Oliver removed his hat and sniffed the air. "That sounds great, and if the aromas in here are any indication, I've come to the right place."

"Yes, sir. My mama makes the best food in the whole territory." The boy nodded. "And I'll see if the cookies have come out of the oven yet."

Oliver blew out a sigh. *Forgive me, Lord.* "Would you like me to wait outside?"

"No, sir. Take a seat right here, and we'll get your meals dished up. Interested in a cup of coffee while you wait?"

"Thank you, but no." The boy's solicitous attitude was a balm to Oliver's raging pulse. "Take your time."

Several minutes later, a buxom woman bustled through a pair of swinging doors carrying a fragrant crate. She set it in front of him with a smile, then whirled and rushed back into the kitchen.

The young man named an amount, and Oliver reached into his pocket. He laid down several coins that included a generous tip, then picked up the wooden box. "I look forward to seeing you again."

His steps were lighter as he left the small restaurant. He should have known better than to ask one of the city's elite where to eat. Lesson learned. He cogitated while he walked. Would the tiny establishment have been any different if the gals had been with him? Was the young man polite because he left Little Doe behind? White men's arrogance knew no bounds, even in the wilds of the Western Territories.

Caroline obviously didn't care about her reputation, but should she? Would her friendship with Little Doe cause her problems down the road? The Indians had been run off their land for the most part, and many who were left were at odds with the settlers. Skirmishes happened regularly, and too many reports of misunderstandings peppered the newspapers. Misunderstandings that resulted in deaths. The sooner he could get the women to their claim and out of town, the better.

In the distance, Caroline's russet hair shone in the sunshine. He quickened his pace and was soon approaching the two women. Her face lit at his appearance, and his breath caught. He blinked and held up the crate, his heart banging against his ribs. "I come bearing gifts."

"Wonderful. There is a grassy area behind the shop at the end of the block." She held up a navy-blue blanket. "And I ducked into the mercantile and picked up our *table*."

"Excellent." He followed them to their picnic location and waited while she spread the cloth. Setting down the crate, he brushed off his hands, then lifted the towel. The savory scent of chicken mingled with the creamy aroma of mashed potatoes. Steaming green beans, corn, and biscuits completed the dinner. He opened a warm package that revealed a half-dozen sugar cookies. His mouth watered, and he extended the parcel. "Hors d'oeuvres, anyone?"

Caroline giggled and snatched one of the cookies. "Definitely."

Little Doe smiled but shook her head.

"Listen, Little Doe." He set down the cookies. "I need to apologize for setting you up to be hurt. It was thoughtless, and I'm sorry."

"No need for that. You are a good man, so you expect the same. I should have known better." She shrugged a slender shoulder. "But I had hope."

"Someday it will be different. Unfortunately, maybe not in our lifetimes, but perhaps our children's lives or their children's."

"Perhaps." She picked up a fork. "For now, we eat together and enjoy one another."

Caroline gave Little Doe a one-armed hug. "And we'll sleep under the stars. It will be a grand way to begin the next chapter of our gold adventure."

Oliver's face fell. Of course. The hotel probably wouldn't allow the Indian woman under their roof. And gentle soul that she was, Caroline had glossed over the fact as if she couldn't wait to spend another night in the open.

Her graciousness was one of the traits he'd miss most when all was said and done.

Chapter Ten

Caroline shivered and burrowed under the blanket. Dampness seeped through the cover, permeating her clothes and chilling her skin. She sighed and pulled down the cloth. Craning her neck, she peeked out from under the wagon. Pink and purple fingers of light streaked the cloudless sky. Further stretching brought the mountains into her field of vision.

Craggy, soaring mountains were frosted with snow even though the calendar had turned to June. At home, the fluffy, white powder would have disappeared from the Georgia mountains weeks ago.

Tears welled in her eyes. Would she ever see the forested ridges again? If so, would she return wildly successful, a rich woman in her own right, or would she be a go-backer? A dismal failure who wasted months of her life seeking elusive glittering flakes and stones.

Footsteps sounded, and a pair of denim-clad legs that ended in scuffed brown boots appeared by the side of the wagon. Oliver. She swiped the moisture from her eyes and cleared her throat. "I hope you're coming to offer breakfast. I'm starving."

He chuckled and squatted down. His tanned face came into view. His hand held a steaming metal cup. He waved his hand, sending the fragrant smell of coffee toward her.

She beamed at him. "That's a good start." She scooted out from under the conveyance, then climbed to her feet, and reached for the cup. Curling her fingers around the warmth, she sipped the dark brew.

"Sleep well?" He cocked his head, a grin tugging at the corners of his mouth.

The coffee curdled in her stomach. Her fingers searched for the ever-present bandanna around her neck, and she cringed. It was pooled around her shoulders rather than hiding the angry, red scars. She tugged the scarf into place, then patted her hair. At least her braid remained in place.

Oliver grabbed her hand and placed it back around the cup. "Stop. You look lovely this morning. Now, let's get some breakfast before it grows cold. Little Doe has pulled out all the stops. She must cook when she's nervous. She's made flapjacks, two kinds of eggs, bacon, and biscuits."

Cheeks roasting, Caroline nodded and stifled the urge to fiddle with her muffler. "That will keep me through lunch."

They turned and walked to the fire where Little Doe hunched over three plates piled with savory food." She smiled at Caroline. "Good sleep? You didn't stir when I got up."

"That's because you're quieter than a mouse." Caroline yawned and sat on the ground near the blaze. "But, yes, I slept well." She took the fork and plate, inhaling deeply. "This smells divine. I'm amazed at what you can do with a skillet and a few embers. The art of cooking eludes me."

"You have other skills." Oliver winked. "Like shooting."

"And driving a team of oxen." She laughed. "But neither of those is any good if I starve to death."

"I would imagine you could get by." His eyes crinkled at the corners, and he popped a piece of flaky biscuit into his mouth. "But I'm sure glad you're here, Little Doe. You're a magnificent chef."

"Chef?"

Caroline nodded. "A fancy French term for cook."

"Not fancy."

"I'll take filling over fancy any day." Caroline bit into a crispy strip of bacon and moaned. "It's like meat candy."

Little Doe snickered. "It's my favorite, too." She finished eating, then rose. "I'll pack the bedrolls."

Oliver shook his head and rose. He scooped his remaining eggs and bacon onto the pancake and rolled the flapjack. "Breakfast on the go. I'll take care of the wagon. You enjoy the fire." He waved one hand, then took a huge bite as he walked toward the vehicle.

"Don't let him get away." Little Doe narrowed her eyes at Caroline. "He is not like most men. He is kind and thinks of others."

"Nonsense." Caroline's pulse tripped. "Neither of us is looking to get married. Yes, he's a nice man, and he's been helpful on the journey, but now that we're here, you and have claims to work. I don't need a husband. You are welcome to him."

"He doesn't look at me like that."

Caroline set down the plate. "Like what?"

"Like a man does when he cares for a woman."

"He's just being polite."

Little Doe snorted a laugh, then laid her empty plate on Caroline's. She spread the embers, then scooped dirt onto the glowing wood until the smoke disappeared. She picked up the soiled dishes. "I'll wash, then meet you at the wagon."

Mind racing, Caroline watched her friend saunter off. Little Doe didn't know what she was talking about. Oliver had been solicitous to her, but he treated everyone with respect. Granted, he seemed to spend more time at their campfire, but he was probably being chivalrous to two women alone. Or perhaps it was Little Doe's cooking.

Bah! Enough time thinking about Mr. Llewellyn. Daylight was burning, and the sooner she got to her claim, the sooner she could prove to her parents she had what it took to be a flourishing prospector.

An hour later, they'd reached her property, set up a tent, and unloaded the equipment. To her surprise, Oliver's tract abutted hers. How had she missed that when they were registering? Had he withheld the information on purpose? Was his presence coincidence? A shiver slithered up her spine. Or had he made a change after getting to know her on the trail? No. That would have involved a lengthy exchange, and his transaction had been as fast as hers.

Her gaze darted to where he and Little Doe crouched by the water. He said something to her, and she ducked her head with a smile. The young woman had come a long way in trusting him since the beginning of the trip. She was still skittish near other men, moving closer to Caroline if someone other than Oliver or the trail boss approached.

The river was crawling with prospectors. Hats crushed low on their heads, they scooped sand into the pan, swirled the water, tipped the container, swirled again, then picked out the flakes. Their sure, steady motions told her they'd been at this for a long while. Weeks? Months?

Their clothes were dirty, worn, and tattered. Based on attire, no one could tell who had struck pay dirt. Would she eventually look like them? She shrugged and smoothed her bloomers. Should she change into the dungarees her mother insisted she pack? No. She might want to work beside the men, but there was no need to look masculine.

Her eyes flicked to Oliver, and she gulped. He was staring at her with a smirk. Could he see her indecision? She returned his smile and straightened her spine, then marched toward them, pan and trowel in hand. "Here goes nothing." She squatted between him and Little Doe, then drove her shovel into the sand.

"Hey, she's not allowed here."

Caroline's head jerked toward the voice.

A burly, bearded man scowled at her from the middle of the water, hands on his hips.

She jumped to her feet. "I am too. This is my claim."

"Not you," he sneered. "Her." He pointed a grimy finger at Little Doe. "We don't want no Injuns."

Beside her, Oliver rose to his full height. He'd dropped his tools, and his hands were clenched into fists.

The man sloshed through the water toward them, and Caroline reached into her pocket for her pistol. Pointing it at him, she said, "I suggest you go back to what you were doing and mind your own business. Who I choose to share my claim with is none of your concern."

"Do you know how to use that thing, little lady? You look too pretty to have the guts to shoot me."

"I wouldn't bet the farm on that, mister," Oliver growled. "There's a man in St. Joseph's who can attest to her abilities." He drew his weapon. "And mine. Now, you take care of your claim, and we'll take care of ours."

The miner held up his hands and shrugged, forehead still creased with a frown. "Fine. But I'm not the only one who thinks she don't belong here." He turned and stomped toward the far bank of the river.

Caroline blew out a deep sigh and stowed her weapon as Oliver tucked his gun in his back waistband. She stuffed her trembling hands into her pockets. She could have handled the codger on her own, but having Oliver's towering presence next to her meant she didn't have to. There was comfort in the thought, but she'd set aside that notion until tonight when she could explore it under cover of darkness.

She raked her gaze over the other miners. No one seemed to be paying her any attention, but the scoundrel made it clear she shouldn't lower her guard. Had she made a mistake in coming? Were her parents right that the wilds of Kansas Territory held too much danger for a woman alone?

Oliver nudged her shoulder and gestured to the stream. "Don't let him get to you. He's a windbag. There's gold to be found."

With a blink, she nodded, then cocked her head. "Shouldn't you be working your own spot? Little Doe and I can do this."

"Maybe tomorrow. I'd like to share your excitement when you find that first nugget."

Her stomach fluttered as she avoided Little Doe's knowing smile.

Chapter Eleven

"Stop trying to marry me off." Caroline huffed a breath at Little Doe. "I'm happy as a single woman, and I don't need some man to tie me down, telling me what to do and how to do it."

"Oliver isn't like that. He treats everyone the same, even women. He talks to me as if I am his sister. Few white men respect women, especially Indians."

"I'm not disagreeing about his behavior, but I'm not looking for a husband, no matter how nice the man is."

Little Doe opened the trunk and pulled out three plates and cups. Frowning, she plunked them on the table with a thump. "Don't be mad."

Hurrying across the tent, Caroline drew the young woman into a quick embrace. "I could never be angry with you, and I know you mean well, but I'm really not interested in getting married." She grinned. "Even to a certain tall, ruggedly handsome cowboy."

"So you admit he is good looking." Little Doe swatted her shoulder. "What else do you think about him?"

Caroline snorted a laugh, then pressed her finger and thumb together and pulled them across her lips. "I'm not saying another word that you'll use against me later."

The tent flap opened, and Caroline looked up as Oliver poked his head inside. Her stomach fluttered, and she tugged at the bandanna around her neck to ensure it was in place. Had he heard any of their conversation?

He removed his hat and held up a pair of squirrels. "I got lucky this morning. Any chance of stew tonight?"

Little Doe held out her hand with a smile. "You bring the meat. You get to pick the meal." She laid the offering in a bowl, then pointed to a pitcher and basin. "Wash up. Breakfast is ready."

He put two fingers to his forehead. "Yes, ma'am."

She giggled and rolled her eyes, then left the tent to tend the meal cooking on the fire outside.

Caroline rubbed her damp palms on her bloomers. "Your timing is impeccable. How do you manage to show up two minutes before breakfast each morning?"

Drying his hands, he winked. "It's a gift."

"More like a sense of smell that rivals that of a bloodhound." Caroline set the utensils on the table, then poured water into three metal tumblers. She dropped into one of the chairs, glad they'd purchased a tent large enough to house an area for dining rather than having to eat all their meals outside regardless of weather.

Little Doe came inside and hefted the Dutch oven onto the table. "Biscuits." Using a towel, she lifted the lid, and aromatic steam rose.

Oliver rubbed his stomach. "My favorite."

The young woman shook her head. "You say that every morning."

He chuckled, then held out her chair. After she sat down with a blush, he lowered himself in the last vacant seat, then held out his hands. "My turn to say grace, ladies."

Despite preparing herself for the feel of his skin against hers, Caroline flinched when their hands connected. A tingle shot from her fingers to her elbow, and warmth filled her stomach. She nibbled her lower lip as she bowed her head. Why couldn't she get used to his touch? Her body responded the same way every morning, rebelling against her conviction that they were nothing more than friends.

"Amen." He released her hand.

She picked up her fork, face heating. So intent on her thoughts, she'd missed the blessing. *Forgive me, Lord.*

"Tell me about your God." Little Doe bit into one of the biscuits.

Caroline gulped and stared at her friend. "What brought this about?"

"I've been thinking for a while. Since meeting you both. You are different, and it seems to be because of your belief in the Great Father. You call him God. I want to know more."

Oliver took a deep drink of water, then sat back. "Do you know anything about Him, Little Doe? Other than what you've seen from us?"

Sadness clouded her eyes. "When I was a little girl, a priest came to our village to tell us about the Great Father. He spoke at one of our gatherings, but his words made some of my people upset. One of the braves killed him before he could finish his stories." She rubbed at a spot on the table. "Like you, he was kind, gentle. He didn't tell us our ways were wrong like most white men. He said he wanted to tell us about his friend Jesus. Before he died, he said he forgave the brave."

"Oh, Little Doe, how awful for you to see that." Caroline squeezed Little Doe's hand.

She shrugged. "The brave thought he was doing the right thing for my people."

"Believers have been martyred through the ages for telling others about salvation." Oliver wiped his mouth. "I'm glad you want to know more. The message is simple, but often difficult to accept because it seems too easy. In a nutshell, God created man and woman who chose to go against Him. He made a tree and told them to leave it alone, but Satan, who used to be an angel in heaven, came to Adam and Eve and convinced them to eat of the tree, that they wouldn't die like God had told them they would."

Little Doe's hand flew to her throat, eyes wide. "They disobeyed the Great Father? Did he kill them?"

"No, but he did banish them from the garden, and their actions separated them from Him. Us, too. We inherited their bad nature, what we call sin."

Tears filled her eyes. "Is that why you are nice to me? So the Great Father will forget your...sin?"

Oliver gave her a gentle smile. "No, He made arrangements for His Son, Jesus, to die for us. But that wasn't the end. Jesus came back to life after three days. When we believe in Him, we want to share His love and the news about Him to others. Like your priest, we chose to forgive people who harm us."

Her brows came together. "My people teach revenge, not forgiving. This is much to think about."

Caroline sighed. Oliver had explained the message beautifully. *Please let his words take root, God. Little Doe needs you.*

Plate empty, Little Doe rose. "I'll clean up, then wash clothes while you go to the river."

"I'd prefer us to stay together, Little Doe." Oliver drained his cup. "No one has said anything or tried to make trouble since that first incident, but we can't let down our guard. How about if we all do the dishes, then take your laundry tub with us. I'll build you a fire, and you can do the clothes there. Is that acceptable to you?"

Oliver gave Caroline an imperceptible nod, and she returned the gesture, her mouth going dry. Little Doe was right. He was different than anyone she'd known, even her father. He offered a suggestion, asking if the solution met the young woman's approval rather than dictating what would happen. Why did he have to be so thoughtful and charming?

"Yes, thank you." Little Doe beamed at him. "I will wash for you, too. Because you help me."

"Oh, you don't have—"

"I want to."

"Okay." He glanced at Caroline.

Her eyes glowed as she met his gaze, and Oliver's chest swelled. She seemed to appreciate his efforts to make things safer for her and Little Doe. A change from the prickly woman who'd scorned him at the beginning of the trip. Over the course of the journey, the wall that surrounded her had slowly crumbled.

She was a complex woman, like none he'd ever met. With Little Doe, she was warm and gracious, the two having developed a close friendship. More than a few times, he'd come upon them giggling like schoolgirls, and they often finished each other's sentences. Proof that people had the same needs and desires no matter what their culture.

In the week since she'd run off the disgruntled miner, there hadn't been any trouble, but he didn't make any assumptions that all was well. However, her manner when she arrived at the river to pan was that of confidence and grit. Her stance dared any of the men to approach or even call out to her. She'd nod at any who bothered to look her way, but she never spoke as she'd prop her rifle in full view, then settle in to work.

Little Doe occasionally hunched beside her, but the young woman's posture was that of a scared rabbit. Her eyes darted back and forth, her neck constantly swiveling as if on the lookout for an escape route. She always seemed much happier doing household chores.

They made quick work of the cleanup, then he created a travois to carry the bucket and clothing bundles. Caroline packed the saddlebags with equipment, and Little Doe placed towel-wrapped packages of food in the tub. She cocked her head at him. "Will the horse be all right? This isn't too heavy?"

Oliver patted Ranger's shoulder. "Ranger's fine. He's a strong fella, but we'll be sure to give him an extra rasher of oats when we return. How's that sound?"

She sighed. "Like a nice treat for him."

"Excellent. You hear that, buddy?" He stroked the horse's muzzle, and the animal nickered. "I'll take that as a yes." He grinned at the women, feeling foolish yet happy. When was the last time he was this carefree? He needed to remember he was on assignment. "Okay, let's mount up."

Thirty minutes later, Caroline was panning, and Oliver tossed the last log on the fire for Little Doe. She waved him off when he asked if she needed his help, so he sauntered to the water's edge. He knelt near Caroline, and a breeze wafted her clean scent of soap toward him. His stomach tightened, and he swallowed. "Uh, what do you think about asking Little Doe if she'd like to earn her own money by taking in laundry?"

"You noticed she's not enamored with hunting for gold?" Caroline sent him a crooked grin.

"Exactly." He hunched into himself. "I know you meant well by sharing the claim with her, and I didn't want you to think I was criticizing, but she seems happiest up to her elbows in hot water."

"Crazy, right?" Caroline snickered. "That's the last chore I ever want to do. If I find enough gold, I'm going to buy new clothes when I need them rather than have to do laundry. I think your idea is good, but only if the men treat her with respect."

"I'll make that clear. I don't want her washing for them to confirm any opinions that she's worth less than they are." He frowned. "She will have the right to refuse any customer."

"Agreed." She nodded and sat back on her haunches. "But I think we should pray about it before asking her. See if God gives us other ideas." She wiped her forehead with the back of a wet hand. "As far as I'm concerned, she doesn't need to do anything to earn her way, but if she's to be independent, she'll need money. I doubt she'll take a handout from me."

"How about if we wait another three days, then we'll talk about this again."

"Perfect." She beamed. "And you did a great job of telling her about Jesus. Better than I could have done. Thanks for caring about her so much."

He cleared his throat. "Of course." Her words warmed him.

Chapter Twelve

Caroline rotated her shoulders to ease the kinks from her muscles. Her hands cramped, and she dropped the pan to flex her fingers. She'd built up stamina over the last ten days, but occasionally her body rebelled.

Sunlight blazed overhead. The unseasonable heat rivaled a July day in Georgia. Perspiration adhered her cotton blouse to her back and pooled under her arms. Droplets formed between her hairline and her hat. She'd given up bonnets for a plains hat to the dismay of Little Doe and Oliver. The stiff brim of the bonnet that shielded her face from the sun blocked her peripheral vision and caused her to constantly swivel her neck like an owl. The movement pulled on her scars and dragged down her bandanna. If women designed clothes, garments would be more practical and less restricting.

She glanced to her right and left. Satisfied no one was looking at her, she removed her scarf and plunged it in the river. She wrung out the cloth, then tied it back around her neck. Sweet relief.

Her stomach rumbled. She'd been panning since shortly after dawn, and the bag tied to her waistband was getting heavy with a mixture of flakes and small nuggets. Combined with her finds from the last two days, the amount meant another trip to the bank where her account was already at a healthy level.

Oliver's claim was producing as well, but he often wandered to her property to chat with her or Little Doe. Several times he'd panned her section, adding to her bulging coffers. She admonished him for not caring about his own claim, but he'd shrug and make some excuse. He also shared their dinner table on a regular basis, a mixed blessing.

"Lunch is ready, Caroline."

Joints popping, she climbed to her feet and trudged to the fire. "Wonderful. I was considering calling it a day."

Little Doe handed her an ironstone plate and a ladle. "You haven't take a day off since starting."

Caroline dunked the dipper into the fragrant concoction and filled her plate. Her mother would be appalled at the amount of food she consumed, but mining gave her the appetite of a field hand. "Vegetable stew? Smells divine."

She sat on a large stone, set the dish on her knees, then said a quick blessing over the food.

Footsteps sounded on the hard-packed ground. Without turning, she knew Oliver approached. Her heart rate quickened, and she pressed her lips together. No matter how many times she reminded herself he was just a friend, her dancing pulse contradicted her.

Little Doe smiled and held out a plate of stew and a spoon. "I made too much as usual. You must help us eat it up."

He took the plate and the utensil, then sat cross-legged on the ground. "You're a life saver, Little Doe." He ate several bites, then said, "Have any of the boys asked you to cook for them in addition to washing their clothes?"

She shook her head. "No, but they are more interested in finding gold than eating. Hard tack and biscuits seem to be all they want." She gestured to a miner at the edge of the river. "Many of them eat while they pan. But I would say no. I don't want to cook for money."

"But the laundry is working out, yes?" Caroline took a swig of water, then gestured to the lines of clothes dancing in the breeze. "You seem to have plenty of customers."

"Yes." Little Doe nodded. "You had a good idea, and the men who hired me say they do not agree with that bad man. Maybe they say that so I will wash and not pan."

"Perhaps, but I watch them with you, and they show respect." Oliver smiled. "Fortunately, not everyone is prejudiced."

Caroline finished her stew and wiped her mouth. "That was delicious, Little Doe. I'm done panning for the day. I'll clean the dishes." She looked at Oliver. "I need to make a trip to the bank. How are your holdings?"

"Enough that I'll join you." His gaze slid to Little Doe. "How much longer are you going to be? I'd like you to accompany us."

She pointed to a large pile of shirts and pants. "I have too much. Mr. Lorrie has been kind to me, like you. I trust him."

Oliver crossed his arms and scanned the activity on the river. "Which one is Lorrie?"

Little Doe gestured to a beefy man with sandy-blond hair who crouched on a rock in the middle of the water about fifty yards away.

He jutted out his chin. "He looks like he can hold his own, but that's awful far."

She put her hand on Oliver's arm. "You could pray to your God to keep me safe while you are gone."

Caroline swallowed a grin as his face flamed. It seemed her friend was close to accepting the Lord. She walked to Spirit and began to saddle the mare. No need to embarrass the man further.

"Turning my words against me, Little Doe? You've learned well. Please forgive me. I don't mean to be overbearing."

"There is nothing to forgive. Now, the day is passing. You must go."

He walked past Caroline and waded into the river to where Lorrie squatted. She watched him bend and speak to the man who nodded. They exchanged a few more words, then Lorrie waved at Little Doe and Caroline. Oliver shook the man's hand and made his way back to shore. "We're all set, but you probably know that."

"Yes, but your concern means much...uh...a lot."

Caroline mounted Spirit and waited for Oliver, who stopped next to Little Doe, bowed his head, and said a short prayer before swinging onto his horse. How did they get so lucky in meeting him on the trail? Or was God watching out for her even though she hadn't asked? An interesting thought she'd explore later.

They rode in silence for a couple of miles, then Oliver said, "We've done well in a short time. What are your plans for your claim?"

"You don't seem as zealous as the other miners." She cocked her head. "Are you getting bored?"

He shrugged. "Wealth has never held great allure for me, and now that I've experienced the tedium of the actual task of panning, I'm not sure how much longer I need to partake."

Her heart fell, but she forced a smile. "It is dull, to be sure, but I will continue for a while longer. I want to be free from depending on my parents." She shifted in the saddle. "Of course, my vein could dry up tomorrow and change my plans. I've heard of that happening to a couple of fellas farther down the river."

"Would you try for another claim or move on?

She studied him. What answer did he want? He seemed to be indicating he was ready to leave, but was he simply feeling out her motives? "I'm growing to love the rugged, wild beauty of this territory. I don't know whether I'd continue to mine, but I don't see myself running home to Georgia either."

They arrived in town and navigated around the hustle and bustle of wagons, carriages, horses, and pedestrians to the bank at the end of the block. Oliver slid from his horse and unbuckled his saddlebags as she did the same. She staggered under the weight, and he hurried around Ranger and took one of her leather sacks. She sent him a grateful smile.

Boots clomping on the wooden sidewalk, they entered the bank and went to the counter.

"Oliver Llewellyn, you old badger. What a surprise to find you here in the middle of nowhere."

Oliver whirled, and his face darkened. He held out his hand. "How are you, Sarge?"

"Right as rain. I'm trying my hand in the gold fields. You?"

Caroline watched the interchange, Oliver's stance stiff and unyielding. Interesting.

"The same." Oliver's voice was monotone.

Sarge looked at Caroline, a wolfish gleam in his eye. "And who might you be?"

She lifted her chin as Oliver said, "Sorry, Sarge. This is Caroline Vogel. Her claim abuts mine. Caroline, this is Sergeant Kane."

"A lady prospector? How novel." Kane winked. "Watch out for this guy; he's a tricky one. Did all our scavenging during the war. Who knows what he'll talk you out of."

Caroline gaped at the man.

"Well, nice to see you, Sarge." Oliver sighed. "Good hunting."

He continued toward the counter, Caroline trotting to keep up with him. There was obviously bad blood between the two. What had happened?

"You, too," the man called from the doorway. "And whatever else you're up to." Kane snorted a laugh. "See you around."

Oliver cringed and avoided her glance.

She gulped. Was that guilt written all over his face? What was he hiding?

Chapter Thirteen

Scowling, Oliver dropped the saddlebags onto the counter. "We've got gold."

The clerk nodded and beckoned for them to go into a room to his right.

Oliver picked the bags and strode to the room, Caroline trotting to keep up. He slowed his steps. "Sorry."

They went inside, and the clerk walked in behind them and closed the door. "I'm Mr. Felden. I will weigh the gold and give you an amount of money equal to its value, signing a statement that you agree to the weight and its worth. Is that clear?"

"Yes." Oliver nodded. "We already have accounts here. I'm Oliver Llewellyn, and this is Miss Caroline Vogel."

"I thought I recognized you, but we have many patrons." Mr. Felden smiled at them over his wire-rimmed spectacles. "Shall we begin?"

Forty minutes later, the transactions were complete, and Oliver pocketed some coins having deposited the rest. Working with the clerk and Caroline had slowed his racing pulse, and the knots in his shoulders had loosened. Ten years had passed since he'd seen Sarge, yet the man could still get under his skin. Eight years a Pinkerton agent, and he'd allowed his emotions to jeopardize a mission. If Caroline's expression was any indication, he owed her some sort of explanation. But what could he say that wasn't a bald-faced lie?

He rose and offered his arm to her. "What's next? Do you need anything at the mercantile?"

She shook her head and tucked her hand in the crook of his elbow. "Truth be told, I'm a bit hungry."

Her warmth permeated his sleeve, sending a jolt all the way to his shoulder. Could she feel that? He cleared his throat. "I could use something to eat, myself. I know just the place." He nodded his thanks to the banker, then opened the door and led Caroline from the room. "And we can talk."

The crease in her forehead smoothed, and she smiled.

Yep, he owed her some sort of explanation. After weeks on the trail getting to Pike's Peak, and then all they'd dealt with after arriving, he had to tell her something. Besides, if he didn't talk about the guy, she'd quiz him unmercifully. She was like a dog with a bone.

They sauntered down the wooden sidewalk to the small restaurant. The same freckle-faced boy stood near the counter, and similar glorious aromas emanated from behind the swinging doors of the kitchen. Oliver lifted his hand in greeting, and the young man smiled, hurrying toward them. "You came back."

"And I brought a friend."

"L-Lovely to meet you, miss." The boy's face reddened to the roots of his hair. "W-We have chicken and dumplings today."

Caroline beamed at him, and the young man bumped into a chair as he led them to a table near the window. Oliver swallowed a grin as they sat down. "That sounds wonderful."

"Absolutely." Caroline nodded.

"B-Be right back." He rushed toward the kitchen, managing to avoid the furniture.

Oliver chuckled. "Someone is smitten by your beauty."

"Stop." She swatted his hand. "It's more likely that he hasn't seen a woman other than his mother in months."

"I—"

"Llewellyn! You again?"

Oliver winced. How had he missed Sarge's entrance? He forced a smile and waved. "Gotta eat somewhere."

"I heard the grub was good in here. You'd know, wouldn't you?"

Sergeant Kane trundled to their table, a lecherous grin on his face. He stared at Caroline and tugged the waistband of his pants over his wide girth. "How nice to see you again, Miss Vogel." He reached for her hand and brought it to his lips.

In his lap, Oliver's hands fisted. Would she see the sergeant for the weasel he was?

She pulled her fingers from his grasp, her face a mask. "Yes."

Grabbing a chair from a nearby table, Kane sat down. "Mind if I join you? I don't know anyone in town yet." He wiggled his eyebrows. "Although that will change soon enough."

"Well—"

"Good." He raised his arm and snapped his fingers, then bellowed. "I'll have what they're having."

The young man sent Oliver a questioning look, and he nodded. Best to get this over with. He doubted the sergeant's presence in the restaurant was a coincidence. How long would it take to figure out what the man wanted?

Kane put his elbows on the table, then leaned toward Caroline. "So, how long you been out here seeking your fortune?"

"Not long." She crossed her arms and pressed against the back of her chair. "Where is your claim located?"

Oliver unclenched his hands. Atta girl, Caroline. Turn the conversation to him.

"Not quite sure. I haven't been to the office yet." Kane puffed out his chest. "I bought it sight unseen, but it's a good one."

"Congratulations."

"Yeah, I'm gonna be rich. I can feel it. Are—"

The young man delivered three steaming plates of food, and Oliver's mouth watered. Perhaps eating would keep Sarge occupied for a while.

"This smells wonderful." Caroline placed the cloth napkin in her lap. "Thank your mother for us."

"Yes, thank you," Sarge's voice boomed, filling the small restaurant.

Dipping his head in acknowledgment, the boy turned and disappeared into the kitchen.

"I didn't get to finish telling you about this guy." Sarge shoveled a spoonful of stew into his mouth, then jerked his head toward Oliver. "He was the best scout I ever saw. He could sneak up close to the enemy without them ever knowing he was there. Saved our necks a bunch of times."

Caroline swallowed and wiped her mouth, curiosity sparkling in her eyes. "You don't say?"

Oliver pushed a dumpling around his plate. How much would the guy tell her?

"Yep. And he kept us supplied, too. Whatever we needed, he found. By hook or by crook." He pointed his fork at Oliver. "Yes, sir. The king of midnight requisitions."

She gaped at him, her spine stiff. "You stole for the army? From whom did you take these items?"

Sarge snorted a laugh and slapped the table. "Anyone and everyone. He even pilfered from the enemy, right under their noses. If you need anything, Llewellyn here is your man." He poked more food into his mouth. "And I could never prove it, but I'm pretty sure he was doing a little spying. Why else would he be so close to the other side?"

Caroline looked at Oliver, and he held her gaze. She broke eye contact, took a sip of water, then turned to Sarge. "He would have to be in order to scout...is that what you called it...for your leaders. Don't you think?"

"Maybe, but I think—"

Oliver forced a chuckle. "Sarge, do you have to talk about me like I'm not here?"

"Sorry, boyo." Sergeant cackled. "You gotta fill me in about what you've been doing since the war. I thought we were gonna keep up, and you vanished. One day you were there, then the next...poof...gone."

"Yeah, I headed home and tried my hand at farming for a bit." Oliver shrugged. "Didn't take to it." As an agent, he needed to be faster on his feet. He was fumbling, and Caroline had to have noticed. If he lied his way out of the conversation, he could probably avert her suspicions, but he struggled with reconciling that part of the job with his faith. Lying was rarely a good solution. Besides, he wanted to be able to look her in the eye. He wanted her respect, even years from now when he was a distant memory for her. "Anyway, I've been kicking around here and there, then I heard about the gold. The stories in the papers make it seem like a sure thing."

"That's what I thought. You, too, little lady?" Sarge nudged Caroline, and her bandanna slipped down. Disgust written on his face, he reared back, then jumped to his feet, an amazing feat for a man his size. "Well, look at the time. I got things to do. Nice to meet you, Miss Vogel. See you around, Llewellyn."

His meal a lump in his stomach, he pushed away his plate. What a disaster.

Chapter Fourteen

"I've had enough." Caroline fumbled the scarf back in place and swallowed past the lump in her throat, then laid her napkin on the table. She'd had more than enough. Enough of Oliver's secrecy. Enough of Sergeant Kane's blathering. And especially enough of feeling less than human because of the ugly scars that marred her appearance. The revulsion on the man's face had cut to the quick. As a former army officer, he would have seen many horrors, yet one look at her puckered skin, and he'd recoiled as if slapped. Run out of her presence as if on fire.

Yet, Oliver remained silent. He'd looked at her with pity, then studied his plate as if seeking secrets of the universe. He was no different than any other man. He'd told her she was pretty, but he obviously didn't mean what he said.

And now she knew he'd withheld information about his past. She thought they'd been open and honest, but there were dark corners within him that he'd failed to enlighten her about. She'd laid herself bare to him, sharing dreams, disappointments, and deficiencies. How foolish she'd been.

Oliver lifted his hand and nodded to the freckle-faced young man.

The boy rushed over and bowed. His brow wrinkled. "Was the stew not to your liking, miss?"

She pressed a hand against her middle. "It was wonderful. I'm...uh...full."

"All right." He picked up the three plates. "Will there be anything else?"

"No, thank you." Oliver frowned. "And apparently I'll be paying for the sergeant's...er...Mr. Kane's meal. How much do I owe you?"

The boy named a figure, and Oliver laid the coins on the table.

Caroline's eyebrow lifted. He'd included a generous tip, evidence of his kindness to those less fortunate. Perhaps, he pitied the café owners, too. Did he think himself above others? Would he ever fully share of himself? She pressed her lips together and rose, the room suddenly stifling. Thanking the young man, she straightened her spine, lifted her chin, and strode toward the door, not caring whether Oliver followed her.

Outside, she squinted at the sun's glare, then tied her bonnet into place. She grabbed the reins from the post and attempted to mount Spirit. Her skirts tangled, and she fell against the horse. Ugh. She'd forgone her usual attire of bloomers and hat for her current socially acceptable garment. She wouldn't make that mistake again.

Bunching the fabric in one hand, she lifted her skirt above her ankles, tucked one booted foot into the stirrup, and swung onto the mare. She huffed out a breath and wheeled the animal away from the restaurant.

The door opened with a bang, and she glanced over her shoulder. Oliver rushed to his horse, yanked the leather traces, then jumped on Ranger. He kneed the animal into a trot and caught up with her. "I'm sorry for what happened back there."

She shrugged. What did he mean? Was he sorry for her humiliation? Or for her realization that he wasn't who he said? What had he done in the war? She leaned forward and urged the mare into a gallop. "Hyah!"

Why did she care what he did during the war? Was being a spy so bad? He'd already told her about being a thief, so she shouldn't have been surprised he used those skills in the army. Had he volunteered, or had he been pressed into the activities by the man who'd recruited him? She knew nothing of war. Was spying worse than stealing? Certainly not worse than killing. And he would have had to kill. She shuddered. Why did men see armed conflict as a solution?

How could she judge him?

Spirit's hooves thundered over the ground. Ranger could easy keep pace, but Oliver let her remain ahead by several yards. Despite his distance, her body tingled as if they sat side by side in the wagon. She imagined his breath on her cheek as he leaned toward her to speak. No! She couldn't think like that. However she felt about him, he would never reciprocate. Never do more than feel sorry for her or think he had to take care of her and Little Doe because they were weak and helpless women. He'd made that clear when he hadn't known what to say in the restaurant.

Tears filled her eyes, and she blinked them away. *Dear God, why did you let me live? You could have taken me home to You after the attack. Now, I am nothing more than an object of pity and horror.*

As was My Son. And worse.

The thought brought her up short as if she'd been doused with a bucket of water. She pulled back on the reins, and Spirit slowed. Caroline had fallen into the chasm of feeling sorry for herself. So what if Oliver never cared for her as more than a friend, perhaps even just as an acquaintance. So what if her appearance was so off-putting that no man would have her. She'd told her parents she didn't need anyone, least of all a husband, yet here she was pining for the loss of a relationship she never had nor attested to want. She was a strong and capable woman. She would work her claim, then figure out where to go from there.

Oliver drew up beside her, his mouth set in a thin line. "I'm sorry for not standing up for you back there. You're upset and have every right to be."

Caroline shook her head. "You don't need to fight my battles for me. I've seen his kind before. Pompous and self-aggrandizing, only surrounding himself with decorations that complement him. I'm thrilled he no longer has any interest."

"But that's not all of it." His voice was quiet. "I see how you look at me. With suspicion. Wondering how much of what he said is correct."

"You already told me about your past. Well, as much as you deem necessary." Her stomach hollowed. "You don't owe me any explanation."

"Yes, I do, but I can't give you one." He blew out a deep breath. "I took an oath never to tell anyone what transpired...what I did. I want to because, if I did, maybe I could shed this awful darkness that overtakes me when I remember."

The wall she'd built around her heart cracked. Just a little. Enough to feel his pain. "A burden shared is a burden lightened."

"Exactly." He gave her a tentative smile. "But I cannot break my vow."

"No. That is not who you are."

"Suffice it to say that mankind needs to find a different way to settle its arguments. Without violence and bloodshed. War is a great waste of life."

"But sometimes the only answer."

He nodded, and they continued on in silence.

She peeked from around her bonnet. He slumped over the horse, his eyes cloudy and distant. Their conversation must have taken him back to the battlefields to relive his secrets, his tender heart no doubt breaking all over again. She understood that he had no choice about his pledge of confidentiality, but what else was hidden behind his façade?

Good thing she'd come to her senses about him.

Chapter Fifteen

Hunched over the water, Caroline's trowel scraped the rocks as she scooped sand from the bottom of the river, then shoveled the gritty mixture into her pan. As she swirled the dish with half-hearted efforts, her gaze strayed to the men scattered across the landscape. Most had grudgingly accepted her; the rest ignored her, more intent on gaining riches than caring that a mere woman had invaded their domain.

Since her arrival, a dozen other women had shown up and been subjected to the same bullying she'd experienced. Ten of the gals remained in the gold fields, their faces masks of determination. She'd visited each one offering support and encouragement, something that would have been nice to receive when she'd come. Or not. Since when did she need accolades from others?

The other two women set up small eateries and had steady clientele, proving that those who provided goods and services to the miners would be the ones to succeed when all was said and done. Perhaps she should give the idea some thought. The hours had to be better, with fewer aches and pains.

She rotated her shoulders to ease the stiffness and caught sight of Oliver farther down the stream. His brimmed hat was pulled low over his forehead, his arms working in rhythmic motions. Scoop. Swirl. Dip. Pick. Repeat. His muscles rippled with his efforts, and her pulse sped up. What would it be like to have those bulging arms wrapped around her?

He must have felt her stare, because he looked in her direction. A smile broke out on his face, and he touched two fingers to his hat brim in silent salute.

Heat suffused her cheeks, and she swallowed as she dropped her gaze. Sunlight glinted off a large nugget, and she huffed out a breath. So intent upon ogling Oliver, she'd almost allowed the golden chunk to slip back into the water. She plucked the ore from the dish and tucked it into the leather pouch at her waist.

Perspiration soaked her bodice, and she pulled the wet fabric away from her skin. She smelled no better than the grizzled men she scorned. She'd proven she could compete with the guys, her bank account expanding by the day. How much longer should she pursue the tedious chore of panning?

The hair on the back of her neck prickled. She raised her head and scanned the horizon. Did danger lurk nearby? The louse, Willis Baldridge, was rotting in jail, but was there still some prospector intent on harming her?

Caroline's eyes fell on Oliver, whose sparkling gray gaze stroked her as if he'd run one of his tapered fingers along her jaw. She shivered and nearly dropped her pan. What was wrong with her? What was wrong with *him*? Fixating on her rather than the task at hand.

She pivoted on her heel, taking him out of her line of vision, but his image floated into her mind. She nibbled on her lower lip as memories washed over her: Oliver seated across the campfire, flames flickering in his eyes as they talked about everything and nothing; Oliver's firm hands helping her onto Spirit; Oliver's towering presence outside the wagon ensuring her safety.

A sigh escaped, and she pressed a hand against her heart. She didn't need a man, but she sure enjoyed having a certain broad-shouldered, ebony-haired one around. Did that mean she'd failed in her pursuit of independence?

Another lump of gold appeared amid the sand and debris. With practiced motions, she fished out the piece and slipped it into the pouch. Cupping the leather bag with one hand, she gauged the weight. Heavy enough to tell her she was done for the day, otherwise, she'd be unable to carry the cumbersome sack to the mare. She struggled to rise, the gold putting her off-balance.

Strong hands gripped her arms and helped her to her feet.

"Hey—" Fists clenched, she whipped her head around.

Oliver released her and held up his hands in surrender, a grin tugging at his lips. "I should know better than to sneak up on you."

She narrowed her eyes, her arms tingling where he'd touched her. "And I should know better than to turn my back on you."

He winked. "Part of this adventure is balancing success with the strength to carry your riches. I've had enough for one day, and the way that strap is digging into your shoulder, I'd say the same for you. Unless you've got a second bag you want to fill?"

"No. I'm done."

"Excellent. I'm just about baked in this sun. Will you let me carry your goods?"

"What's the catch?" She snickered. "There's always a catch."

Pressing his hands to the sides of his face, he widened his eyes in exaggerated shock. "I'm hurt you'd think that."

"Right."

Laughter rumbled from his chest. "You cook me dinner."

"You have to build the fire."

"Otherwise, we might never eat."

"Funny. Do we have a deal?" Caroline swallowed. *Please say yes.*

"Of course." He engulfed her hand in his and shook it, with the seriousness of a diplomat sealing a treaty.

Goose bumps covered her arms, and she extricated her palm, then pulled the leather band over her head and gave him the pouch.

Oliver cradled the bag, then pretended to stagger. "Impressive."

She swatted him. "You doubt my capabilities?"

"Only a fool would do that." With a smirk, he twisted away, and his boot caught a boulder. He yelped and hurled headfirst into the river. The bag fell from his hands and submerged with a splash. His hat popped off and danced downstream on the current. His face the color of her mother's burgundy drapes, he hauled his drenched form to his knees, then bent to retrieve her pouch. "Speaking of capabilities..."

Caroline swallowed a giggle. He was embarrassed enough without her laughing at him, but the temptation clawed at her.

His gray eyes gleamed with humor. "You didn't have to push me."

"I didn't pu...oh...you're kidding." She leaned forward and grabbed his hand. "Here...let me help you." Losing her balance, she pitched forward and landed beside him, water soaking through her clothes. "Oh!"

He roared with laughter. "Seems like it might be a good thing that we're done working."

She was close enough to see the ivory-colored flecks in his eyes. A light breeze wafted his scent of leather, perspiration, and the unique essence associated with him, toward her. She fought the urge to inhale. Even in his chagrin, he could poke fun at himself and lighten her mood with his antics.

Would it be so bad to be married? To him? She pressed her lips together. As if he actually wanted her.

Chapter Sixteen

Oliver's heart banged in his chest. Hair hanging in bedraggled red ropes down her back, Caroline never looked more beautiful. Her eyes sparkled like emeralds, and her face glowed. The wall she hid behind seemed to be gone as she laughed. He grinned at her like a lovesick puppy. "This is a fine mess, isn't it?"

Hands wrapped around her middle, she nodded as she worked to catch her breath. "S-So m-much for helping you."

"It's the effort that counts." He chuckled. "Now, we need to get out of these sodden clothes before we catch our death." He scrambled to his feet, then bent and swung her over his shoulder.

She shrieked and wriggled.

He chuckled as he waded out of the water, then set her down on the dry ground. "You can holler at me in a minute. I need to find your gold." He pivoted and peered into the water. Where...ah, there. He snatched the bulky pouch from the depths and slung the strap over his head, then grabbed his own bag.

With one hand on her hip, she wagged her finger at him. Her efforts to look stern were ruined by her saucy smile and shining eyes.

In a fluid motion, he looped his arm through hers and turned her toward the horses. "Your attempt to appear forbidding would be more convincing if you didn't seem to be having such a good time."

Her breath whooshed out, and she chortled. "I can never stay angry at you."

"And for that I'm grateful." He winked, then put down the bags and cupped his hands to help her onto Spirit. Caroline swung into the saddle, her soggy skirts slapping him in the face. He sputtered, then retrieved the satchels and stuffed them into the pommel bag in front of her. He went to Ranger and untied his bedroll. Shaking out the worn blanket, he handed it up to her. "Wrap this around you."

"But—"

"The sooner we head out, the sooner we get to your place." Oliver mounted Ranger and wheeled the animal away from the river. He nudged the horse into a cantor, enough speed to make good time without creating a wind that would send chills through his skin.

Seconds later, Caroline caught up with him, an abashed look on her face. "Thank you for the covering."

"Any time." He shrugged. "You want to be independent. I get that, but I'm a fixer. I see a problem, and I try to solve it. You were wet. I had a blanket. And before you say that I'm wet, too, I was raised to think of others first...yes, women, but all people."

"Point taken." Her fingers tightened on the reins, and she ducked her head. "I'll try not to be so stubborn."

"I prefer to think of you as...uh...strong willed, and it's what gotten you this far." His stomach rumbled. "Now, I'm starving. That little dunk in the river has delayed lunch."

"As you wish." She leaned forward and kneed the mare. "Hyah!" The horse shot forward like a bullet from a gun. As they disappeared into the woods, Caroline's laughter faded.

He guffawed and urged Ranger into a gallop. The air sliced through his soggy shirt and pants like needles, and he shivered. He shivered and crouched over the horse's neck. The animal's legs ate up the distance, and Oliver soon saw Caroline in the distance, bedroll flying out behind her. "Don't let her get away." Ranger surged forward.

She glanced over her shoulder, and her jaw dropped.

"Didn't expect me to catch you, did you?" he shouted as Ranger drew close to Spirit.

With a light touch on the reins, she slowed her horse to a trot. "Just wanted to give you a challenge."

He pulled alongside and chuckled. "How is that different from any other day?"

"Hey—"

"Kidding. I'm kidding." They reached the edge of the clearing. "Let's hope Little Doe has a fire going."

Her teeth chattered as she nodded and tucked the blanket under her chin.

They wended their way through the tents until they arrived at Caroline's. He jumped down and hurried to her side. She tossed him the blanket, then slid to the ground. Before he could change his mind, he wrapped an arm around her shoulder and led her to the fire that was little more than embers. She fit perfectly against him, her head coming just to his chin. "We...uh...fell in the river. Can you get her dry clothes? I'll build up the blaze."

Little Doe's raised eyebrow spoke volumes.

His face warmed, and he released Caroline. Why did he feel like he was in the schoolmaster's office?

"Come." Little Doe looped her arm with Caroline's, and they headed inside the tent.

He poked at the glowing coals, and sparks shot into the air. He added a couple of pieces of wood, then blew deep breaths over the pile. Tiny flames flickered, then grew as they licked at the dry logs. He rubbed his hands together and crouched closer.

The tent flap opened, and Caroline appeared dressed in dungarees and a flannel shirt, the ever-present bandanna tied around her neck like an ascot. She'd toweled her hair, so it was only damp, the tresses curling around her face and dangling to her waist.

His pulse quickened. How could she be dressed like a man, yet look like a princess?

She jerked her thumb toward the tent. "Little Doe is seeing if we've got anything to fit you."

"I doubt it, but thanks for trying." He hunkered closer to the fire. "My front is nearly dry."

Her gaze flicked to his chest, then she looked away, her cheeks pink. "The deal was for me to cook dinner."

Little Doe exited the tent carrying a basket filled with clothes. "I must deliver finished laundry. Do you wish me to go to your tent for a shirt?"

"I should come with you." He climbed to his feet, then noticed a young man standing a few yards away. Squaring his shoulders, Oliver narrowed his eyes. "What do you want?"

The young man yanked off his hat, his face red. "I'm...uh...I...um...came to help Miss Little Doe. Carry the clothes so she doesn't have to."

Oliver looked at Little Doe. "This true?"

"Yes." She blushed. "Ned is nice. He will keep me safe."

He glowered at the boy. "See that you do."

"Yes, sir." Ned clamped his hat back on, then reached for Little Doe's load. They turned and walked away.

"How long has *that* been going on?"

Caroline smiled. "A few days. He seems smitten."

"He's barely out of short pants." Oliver stuffed his hands into his pockets. "Can he defend her?"

"The boy made it to Pike's Peak in one piece and has been here for months. I'd say he's got what it takes." She gestured toward the campfire. "Quit worrying, and get that ready for cooking."

"Yes, ma'am." He knelt near fire and used a stick to rearrange the logs. "By the time you're ready, we should have a good bed of coals."

They worked in silence for several minutes, Oliver watching Caroline from the corner of his eye. She was so graceful, even doing mundane chores like fixing food. The setting sun glinted off her hair, setting the curly locks ablaze. His mouth dried. What would it be like to run his hands through the tresses? Were they as soft as they appeared?

"Okay. I'm ready."

"What?" He blinked.

"Dinner is ready to go on the fire." She tilted her head and pointed to the lidded pot filled with root vegetables. "You okay?"

"Yeah, just woolgathering." He swallowed and stood. She must think him a fool. "A good bed of coals on this side."

Caroline buried the wrought-iron pot into the embers, then used a metal pan to scoop additional coals on top. She tossed the pan onto the table where it landed with a clang. She brushed her hands together, then turned. Her foot caught a stone on the ground, and she stumbled. Arms pinwheeling, she fell forwarded against his chest with a grunt.

His arms went around her, and he marveled at how well she fit into his embrace. Their faces were inches apart. Her breath stroked his cheek as she stared at him, green eyes wide and searching. His gaze went to her mouth. So close. So inviting.

He bent his head and pressed his lips on hers.

Chapter Seventeen

Caroline's heart thundered against her ribs as she melted against Oliver. His end-of-day whiskers brushed her chin, sending shivers up her spine. Her arms snaked around his waist, and she pulled him closer. His fingers drew lazy circles on her back, and her toes curled. A sigh escaped. She loved how safe and special he made her feel.

Wait. Love?

Face hotter than a blacksmith's fire, she pulled away, then lowered her gaze. She whirled, then fell to her knees near the iron pot. She couldn't love him. That would mean she needed him. "I...uh...better check on dinner."

Behind her, he cleared his throat. Then silence. He obviously didn't know what to say. Would he apologize for the kiss? Say it was a mistake? Tell her he didn't mean it?

She grabbed a stick, slid it through the handle, and lifted the lid. *Dear God, this changes everything. Now what?* The vegetables had barely cooked, but she made a fuss stirring and rearranging them in the pot. Anything to prevent her from looking at Oliver. Risking the look regret or pity in his eyes. Because he couldn't possibly care for her. Not like a man who would want to marry.

Her stomach hollowed, and she dropped the lid onto the pot with a clash. She scrambled to her feet. "I...uh...forgot something in the tent." Eyes averted, she rushed past him.

"Caro—"

"I'll be back." She ducked inside the shelter and touched her lips. They felt the same, yet different. How was that possible? Her legs trembled, and she sank onto the bed, a canvas stretched over a simple wooden frame.

How had he infiltrated her heart? She'd been so careful all these years, but she'd let down her guard, and now she couldn't imagine her world without him. His image floated into her mind, gray eyes that crinkled at the corners and morphed from silver to slate to gun metal depending on his mood. Ebony hair that shimmered blue-black in the sun. Broad shoulders on his towering form that made her feel petite despite her five-foot-ten-inch height.

Raking her fingers through her hair, she slumped. Yes, he was handsome, but it wasn't just his looks that drew her. His kindness to her, but mostly how he treated Little Doe. Like an equal, someone who had value. And his faith put her own to shame. His confidence in God seemed unshakeable, whereas she constantly questioned the Lord, railed against him when she wasn't getting her own way.

Besides, at some point, he would tire of searching for gold and head off. Based on what she'd seen today, his leaving might be sooner rather than later. He was a man of action, and huddling over the river swirling a pan was hardly challenging for him.

Pain stabbed at her heart, and she rubbed her chest. The void when he left would be huge. A gaping chasm, but she would force herself to forget him. To chalk up her foolishness at falling in love to experience and move on to the next chapter in her own life.

"Yeah, right." She rose and paced the small enclosure. Four steps. Turn. Four steps. Would it be so bad to have a husband? One who cherished her and wasn't arrogant or prideful? One whose eyes lit up when she entered the room?

Too bad that would never happen. She was ugly. No man could see past her scars. Even her parents knew she was unattractive. They never said as much out loud, but she saw it in their eyes, in the actions. And unsightly women did not find men willing to marry them.

Perhaps he'd kissed her out of loneliness. After all, the few women in the area were either married or prostitutes, and a man has needs, or so her mother would say.

Enough! She needed to get a grip on her emotions. One simple kiss, and she was a tangled mess. It probably meant nothing to him. She'd stalled long enough. Dinner would be scorched, her inability to cook another reason for him to look at her with pity.

She shoved opened the flap and stepped outside.

Oliver looked up, eyes twinkling. "Find what you were looking for?"

"No, but it doesn't matter." She gulped. What would he say when she told him she was looking for answers? "Thanks for keeping an eye on the food. It should be read—" She gaped at the blanket lying on the ground with plates, cups, and utensils set as if on a table. A jar filled with wildflowers sat in the middle next to the Dutch oven. A jar? Where had he found that? And what did he mean by all this?

Confusion, shyness, and suspicion mingled on Caroline's face, and Oliver swallowed a grin. She'd been disconcerted by the kiss. Fleeing red faced into the tent had told him that. The question was whether she'd been more upset that he'd kissed her or that she'd responded. Because respond she did. With unreserved passion.

He dished a generous helping onto the metal plates. "Yes, dinner's ready. Make yourself comfortable."

She hesitated, then settled on the ground and picked up her fork. She pushed a potato chunk around the dish. "It was a mistake." She poked the food into her mouth and chewed, her gaze ricocheting around the area, looking at everything but him.

"Letting you cook?" He scooped up some of the vegetables. "Don't be silly. It's delicious."

"That's not what I meant." She laid down her fork and wrung her hands. "The kiss. It was a mistake. I never should have—"

"You didn't...well, you did...but I initiated it." He cocked his head, his pulse pounding. "Why do you think it was a mistake?"

"We're friends. Good friends." She plucked at the fabric of her dungarees. "Which has been surprising, truth be told. I've never had a friend who was a man. But I've told you things I haven't shared with anyone else. And you've taught me a lot...about being on the trail and being safe." She finally met his eyes. "And about God. I'm grateful for that."

"Grateful?" His heart clenched.

"Yes." She nodded. "I appreciate all you've done for Little Doe and me, especially Little Doe. You treat us both like intelligent people, which few people do for a woman, let alone an Indian. You have more integrity in your little finger than most men have in their entire body."

"Hardly." He frowned. If she knew he was being paid to watch out for her, she'd change her opinion about him. "There are things—"

"No one's perfect, but give yourself credit for being an upright man." Caroline gave him a tremulous smile. "And you deserve a wife to keep you company, and you should pursue Little Doe."

He widened his eyes. "What?"

"Little Doe is beautiful and strong and skilled. I don't think she wants to go back to her tribe, and she'll need a husband."

His mouth twisted. "She has no interest in me. Didn't you see how she and that young man looked at each other?"

Caroline shrugged. "Then maybe advertise for one of those mail-order brides. You could list exactly what you want."

"You've said nothing of love."

"That would come...eventually." She fiddled with her bandanna, drawing it close to her chin. "Or so I've been told."

He picked up the cup and took a long drink. He didn't want to be just friends. He knew that now. He wanted to yank off her scarf and free her from the confines of thinking she needed to cover her damaged skin. She'd been hurt by shallow and ignorant people. He wanted to chase away the clouds in her eyes and bring a smile to her lips. He wanted to tackle every day with her by his side.

How could he convince her? Would telling her outright scare her off? Would he awaken to find she'd packed up and skedaddled? "Look, here's the thing. I don't think it was a mistake." He paused, watching her process his words, then plunged in: "I'm going to lay it out straight, and I'd like you to consider what I'm about to say. Pray about it. Talk to Little Doe. Will you do that?"

"Okaaay." Skepticism colored her voice.

"Thank you." He blew out a deep breath. "You think you are unlovely. That your physical scars make you ugly. And, unfortunately, some people only see the outside of a person and have made you believe those lies with their reactions."

Tears welled in her eyes, and she blinked them away.

"But as God's creation, you are special, unique. You are gracious, gentle, and clever. Smart as a whip, yet you never make others feel dumb. You're tenacious and will do whatever is necessary."

"Those are all internal characteristics. You failed to mention my appearance. Even you can't admit I'm disfigured."

He reached for her hands, but she pulled herself out of reach. He leaned closer and captured her fingers. "You didn't let me finish. Are your scars hard to look at? Sometimes, because they bring to mind a terrified little girl who experienced a horrific attack. But they also remind me of your bravery. Your fight to live afterwards. I wish you could believe that you are an incredible woman, Caroline, on the inside *and the outside*. Now, I've said enough. Let's enjoy each other's company and the food." He released her hands. "I'm thinking this is the last time you're going to cook if you can help it."

She gave him a wobbly smile, then straightened her spine. "You've got that right."

Oliver lifted his cup in mock salute, then drank to hide his frown. Was it time to tell her that her parents had hired him, or should he wire them and tender his resignation?

Chapter Eighteen

The wagon creaked to a stop, and Caroline jumped to the ground. Three days had passed since her fateful kiss with Oliver, and the awkwardness between them had begun to dissipate. After a pair of miners stumbled into her tent this morning, she'd gone to town, taken some of her hard-earned money, and purchased materials to construct a cabin. The entire building wouldn't be much larger than her bedroom in Georgia, and not nearly as luxurious, but lots warmer than the tent, and she could put a lock on the door.

She'd grabbed her rifle that she kept by the bed, and the men had hightailed it out of the tent faster than a bobcat on the hunt.

It seemed the more men who arrived and the more successful they became, the rowdier their behavior. At the end of the day, a large number of them mounted up, nugget-filled bags in hand, and headed into Boulder City where they wasted their takings on liquor and women. Sometime after midnight, they'd return to the tent city, drunk, rambunctious, and rude. Oliver's tent was nearby, but she needed to be able to handle situations on her own. He wouldn't be close forever.

Raucous laughter split the air, and she glanced at a pair of miners crouched over a campfire in front of a tent, if one could call it that. A torn and dirty canvas was draped over a handful of stakes the height of a man. Barely enough coverage to keep out the elements. One of the men drank from a flask, then nudged his companion and said something that sent them into another round of hilarity.

She raised an eyebrow and shook her head. Her mother's warnings had proven to be correct over the last several days. It was a wonder she and Father hadn't put up more of a fight about Caroline making the journey. If she had a daughter, she might not be so acquiescent. She hadn't believed herself to be sheltered or naïve, but the activities of the men had sent her scurrying into the tent on more than a few occasions. Yes, a lock on a solid wooden door would be welcome.

"I don't mean to judge, but I've never understood man's need to drink himself into oblivion." Oliver hoisted a stack of boards out of the wagon bed

Tearing away her gaze from his bulging muscles, she swallowed and picked up the sack of nails. "Me neither, but the men at home who did it seemed to be trying to forget bad memories or take a break from a hard life."

"Good point, but these men are pulling in gold. What's to forget?"

She shrugged as she carried the pouch to where he'd piled the wood. "If you're asking me to help you understand why men do things, you're talking to the wrong person."

"Fair enough." He chuckled and went back to the wagon for another stack. "I'm glad you've decided to erect a cabin."

"That decision was made for me." She tsked. "Fortunately, I didn't have to shoot either of the men to convince them to leave."

"I've been spreading the word about the incident, mostly about your abilities with a weapon. Hopefully, this group will think twice about trying to get into the cabin."

"They were so inebriated, they thought it was their tent."

He finished stacking the wood, then rubbed his hands together. "Let's get to it."

"Thanks for helping. Little Doe has more laundry customers, so she's busy. I couldn't figure out how I was going to keep ahold of the boards and nail them into place." She grinned. "And you don't have to worry about me cooking as your reward. Little Doe was so excited to hear we were getting a real house, she's offered to cook for you all week. And do your laundry."

With a chuckle, he picked up a hammer. "Glad to be giving a hand. I'm not sure it will be a real house, but it will be sight better than that tent."

"Tell me the truth." She sent him a wicked smile. "You're happy not to be at the river hunched over a pan."

Throwing his head back, Oliver guffawed. His eyes twinkled, and he winked. "You know me too well."

Her face warmed. His teasing always made her feel fuzzy inside. What was that all about? She reached for the other hammer so she could compose herself. He didn't need to know he was getting under her skin. That she'd begun to take his words to heart—that perhaps she did have value no matter what she looked like. That God had saved her from the animal for some reason, one that she might never know.

She hadn't talked to Little Doe yet, but she'd been praying like he'd asked. Being truthful with God as she'd never been. There'd been anger. Lots of anger and words good girls didn't use, but somehow she knew He was glad she'd finally been honest with her feelings. She still had times of resentment and jealousy of Little Doe and her gorgeous bronze skin, silky black hair, and chocolate-brown eyes, but those moments were fewer. And it certainly wasn't the young woman's fault God has blessed her with such beauty.

"I've removed the pegs. The next step is to pull out the stakes," Oliver's voice rumbled.

Dropping the hammer, she pivoted. He must think her a complete dolt. She'd been so caught up in her thoughts, she'd been useless. "Uh, thanks." She grabbed the nearest wooden picket and yanked it out. The canvas collapsed, and she moved to the next pole. Then the next.

He took care of the other side, and soon the heavy fabric was flat on the ground. With a few quick motions, he folded the tent into a small bundle.

"You've done that more than a few times."

His eyes took on a distant gaze. "We learned to break down at a moment's notice. One of the actual useful skills left over from the war."

"I didn't mean to bring up bad memories."

"Not your fault. Sometimes the simplest action can bring them to the surface. This happens to be one of them." He snapped his fingers. "I need to run back to my place for a minute. This is going to be hot work, and I left our canteens there. Won't be but a minute."

She nodded as he trotted off, then studied the pile of wood. Rough and uneven, the boards would probably gap in places, but she'd be gone by the time winter rolled around. She wasn't desperate enough for gold to linger during the brutally cold and snowy months of the mountains.

"Hey, little lady."

Caroline whirled, and her stomach clenched. Dirty, unkempt, and smelling of liquor, one of the men who'd barged into her tent sauntered toward her, a leer twisting his lips. She shook her finger at him. "Don't you dare come any closer."

"You ain't got that fancy rifle with you this time."

Her knees trembled, but she drew herself to her full height, a good six inches over the man. "No, but that doesn't mean I can't defend myself."

He barked an ugly laugh. "Just because you dress like a man, doesn't mean you're as strong as one." He grabbed her arms in a viselike grip. "Women like you need to be taught a lesson. Taught you don't belong in the gold fields." His foul breath stroked her cheek.

Gagging, she swallowed against the nausea that threatened. Oliver appeared among the tents behind him, and she nearly fainted with relief. She only needed to hold on for a few more seconds.

Face in a stonelike mask, eyes dark as flint, Oliver crept toward them on the balls of his feet. He reached out and jerked the man by the scruff of his neck, then tossed him to the ground. "You're lucky I don't shoot you. Or perhaps I should let her do it."

Mouth working like a fish out of water, the man threw up his hands. "I was just playin' with her. Didn't mean nothing."

"Nice try. You're lying. Now, go to whatever rock you crawled out from under, grab your things, and get out of camp."

"You can't tell me—"

"Consider it a suggestion. Justice is meted out quickly in the camps, most times without due process, and once the men hear you attacked this nice young lady, well..." He shrugged. "But you're welcome to stay and take your chances."

"Gold is almost played out anyway," the man snarled. He jumped to his feet and shook his fist at the two of them. "Someday your high-and-mighty ways aren't going to work, and you'll get what's coming to you." He raced between the tents and disappeared from view.

Caroline swayed on her feet, dots of light piercing her vision. "Thank you for coming to my rescue." Her voice trembled in her ears. She'd be on her own once Oliver moved on. Not that she couldn't learn to pack a pistol and be prepared to defend herself, but she no longer wanted to be on her own. She wanted Oliver by her side. Forever and always. Too bad it wouldn't happen.

Chapter Nineteen

Rain thrummed against the roof, and thunder rocked the tiny cabin. Oliver squinted at the checkerboard in the dim lantern light. "It wasn't exactly a barn raising, but we did get your place built in a hurry."

Caroline smiled at him from across the table. "Days like today make me appreciate my folks' home. Snug, warm, and bright, no matter the weather." She jumped two of his pieces and landed on a square at the edge of the board. "Crown me, " she said as she picked up the black discs. She cleared her throat. "Thanks again for saving me from harm."

"Little Doe confirmed that he's gone...left camp. Sold his claim and skedaddled." He placed a red disc on top of her piece, then slid one of his checkers forward. "Why did she move back into a tent? I thought she was looking forward to being in a house, such as it is."

"Said the tent was more spacious." Caroline shrugged. "I think there's more to it than that, but much as I questioned her, that's all she'd say. I worry about her alone in the midst of all those tents inhabited by men."

"Ned Thaxton has been keeping an eye on her. He seems to be a good lad, and though young, the men know not to cross him."

"Maybe she's caught between two worlds." Her forehead wrinkled. "She's made it clear she won't try to find her tribe, but many of her ways aren't like ours. And she often seems uncomfortable. Like being in the cabin. Did you notice how she seemed to watch the walls during dinner last night, as if she expected them to move. She tossed all night, then moved out at first light."

"Perhaps being inside a building is too reminiscent of the years she was trapped with Willis Baldridge. Bad memories associated with walls and a door."

Caroline's green eyes clouded, and she moved a checker. "How awful if that's true."

He nodded and tried not to stare. Caroline had braided her hair into a long rope that hung down her back, but several strands had sprung free and curled around her head. Her alabaster skin shone as if lit by a beacon. He blinked. Alabaster? Since when did he start thinking like a poet?

Oliver slid a piece forward. He could relate to feeling caught. Resolute that he needed to come clean with Caroline about her parents' role in his presence, he couldn't bring himself to make the confession. As soon as he did, everything would change. She'd hate him for his subterfuge. Throw him out of her life like yesterday's trash.

She was feeling better about herself. He hadn't followed up on their conversation. It felt too much like prying, but she didn't fiddle with her bandanna nearly as often, and her eyes had lost their haunted appearance. God was working in her life, but unfortunately Oliver wouldn't be around to see her fully healed. She'd run him off long before then.

Leaving a gaping hole where his heart had been.

"You okay?" She cocked her head. "Seems like you've been arguing with yourself."

He forced a laugh and waved his hand in a dismissive gesture. "I was, but it ended in a tie."

"I've had those kinds of disputes. Give it some time. The answer usually presents itself." She pointed to the board. "Meanwhile, you need to crown me again."

Work itself out? Only if you could call being shunned with disgust by the woman he loved a solution. Not the one he hoped for. Would she let him tell his side of the story? That he didn't mean to fall in love with her. He'd guarded plenty of women in his time with Pinkerton, but none had affected him like Caroline. Her grit, gumption, and graciousness combined with emerald-green eyes that snapped with intelligence and porcelain skin that begged to be stroked.

Stop!

"Still arguing with yourself?" She smirked and jumped one of his checkers. "Better pay closer attention to the game, or you're going to lose at both."

Oliver snorted a laugh. She had that right. He crossed his arms and leaned back in the chair. "So what are you going to do when you've had enough of the glamorous life of prospecting? Or when your claim gives up its last flake?"

She rubbed her jaw. "There must be other places in the States and territories that have gold. Or maybe silver. There was Georgia, then California, and now Pike's Peak."

"You enjoy backbreaking work, do you?"

"The rewards anyway. Not necessarily financial, although the money is nice to give me independence, but the knowledge that I did this. I trekked hundreds of miles, dug some gold, and built a house. All things I've never done before."

"You've much to be proud of. You must be close to becoming a woman of means. Wealthy enough not to have to work ever again." He crossed his legs. "And you've proven yourself as you'd hoped. Wherever you go, you'll be able to build a mansion and hire a cadre of servants. Become a woman of leisure once you tire of digging in the soil."

"I'd go crazy sitting around." She twisted her lips. "I could go back to teaching, I guess."

"Your tone of voice tells me that's not your first choice." He grinned. "Or even your last. You could do anything you set your mind to. What is it that excites you? Challenges you? *Besides* panning for gold."

"Hmm. Good question." She wrinkled her forehead and pursed her lips.

Her very kissable lips. Oops. His gaze shot to the checkerboard to discourage the thought, but the memory of her in his arms, her graceful form pressed against his chest, washed over him. He tugged at his collar. "This tiny place sure holds in the heat."

"Yes, quite cozy." She smiled. "Hardly a mansion, but it's perfect."

His eyes went back to her mouth. "So...uh...you didn't answer the question."

"Promise you won't laugh?"

"Of course not."

"I think I'd like to do something to help the Indian women and tell them about Jesus. I'm not sure how, but I feel a...I don't know...a pressure when I think about them." She fiddled with one of the checkers lying next to the board. "Does that sound foolish?"

"Not in the least. We...uh...could search out churches that might have relationships with the tribes...on the reservations."

"Do you think they hate us?" She frowned. "Would they even want to hear from me?"

"Everyone needs friends, and that's the best place to start." He laced his fingers together, game forgotten. "You offered your friendship to Little Doe. Then you were able to share your faith. One step at a time." He sighed. Why did he think he deserved a woman like Caroline? Yes, he'd been forgiven and, according to the Bible, was a new person, but his past would be an impediment to anything she tried to do, especially when she reentered society. They'd want nothing to do with a woman who had a jailbird for a husband. And they'd find out. Maybe not right away, but somehow, in some way, his past would catch up with him...and her.

It was time to go. He'd head to town in the morning and send a telegram to her parents and Pinkerton. The sooner they found a replacement agent, the better.

Chapter Twenty

"Mother! Father!" Caroline's voice squeaked as she stood with her hand on the doorknob and gaped at her parents. "How—"

They beamed at her in the early morning light. Her mother pulled her into a tight hug. "We wanted to see how you were doing. You haven't written in a while."

"But to come all this way. How did you get here?"

Father squeezed her shoulder. "Are you going to leave us standing on the threshold?" He wore a sloppy grin.

"N-No. I'm sorry." She stepped back and widened the door. "There's not much room in here, but it will give us privacy."

She gestured to the table and chairs. "Would you like to have a seat? I could make some coffee."

They dropped onto the rustic seats, and Mother shook her head. "We thought we'd take you to breakfast, then come back and help you pan." She rubbed her hands together. "It's been almost thirty years, but I think I remember how."

Father chuckled and kissed her cheek. "Always the adventuress."

"One of the many reasons you love me." Mother nudged his shoulder, then folded her hands. "I'm thrilled you have a cabin. Complete with a wood floor. The claim must be doing well."

"Yes, it is, but wait...you didn't answer my question about how you traveled."

Mother shrugged. "We took the train and shipped the carriage and horses with us. Like you, we took the train to St. Joseph, then used the conveyance to hopscotch our way between local trains, cutting the trip in half. We arrived late yesterday afternoon. We're staying at the Grand."

"You could have sent a telegram." Caroline narrowed her eyes. "Why did you really come?"

"We were worried." Mother's bottom lip poked out. "You promised to write."

Caroline crossed her arms. "I'm not buying it, but I guess I'll find out eventually."

Father gazed around the room. "Seems well-built even though some of the boards are warped. Must keep out the elements for the most part." He turned to her. "I am glad you're not in a tent, and there is a lock between you and those ruffians."

"We finished it a few days ago. It has been nice to sleep under a roof."

"We?" He cocked his head.

"Oliver Llewellyn. I mentioned him in my letters. His claim is not far, and he's been a big help to Little Doe and me."

"I'll have to meet this young man of yours."

Her face warmed. "He's just a friend. But I'm sure he wouldn't turn down a free breakfast."

"Will you need to change, or is Boulder City so wild no one will blink at your bloomers?"

"I purchased a split skirt. That way I can ride without a side saddle."

"Excellent." Father climbed to his feet. "Tell me which tent is his, and I'll get him."

"Well...uh...shouldn't I introduce you?"

He went to the door. "Nonsense. I have to test this man's mettle."

"Okay. He's three tents over."

"I'll go with you." Mother jumped up, and they left the cabin.

Caroline shook her head and stared at the empty space where her parents had been moments ago. They were up to something. What was it? To travel fourteen hundred miles on a whim wasn't their style.

She rose and went to her trunk, then opened the lid and pulled out the yellow split skirt she'd splurged on during their last trip to town. Truth be told, she was tiring of the bloomers and the frowns she received when wearing them. The skirt gave her mobility, yet she still felt like a woman. Her pulse tripped. Oliver seemed to prefer them, too.

"Stop." She rubbed her forehead, then quickly changed her clothes. She tossed the bloomers onto the cot, then grabbed her reticule. The less time her parents had alone with Oliver, the better. She rushed out of the cabin to find the threesome waiting by the horses. "Well, that was fast."

Father chuckled. "You were right about the free breakfast. Let's mount up. I'm ravenous."

Oliver touched the brim of his hat. "Morning."

"Good morning." She pressed her lips together and climbed onto Spirit. Oliver's eyes were clouded. What had transpired between her parents and him? She kneed the horse into a trot, and he fell in beside her. Her parents rode behind them.

The short journey into town was silent, and they enjoyed a hot meal at Kate's Grille during which her mother had held court like a society matron. They were now window-shopping along the main thoroughfare. Oliver and Father walked ahead, while she and Mother sauntered past the displays, tarrying when they saw items of interest.

Mother stopped and pointed to an ornate bonnet at the millinery. "Seems a little much, don't you think?" She glanced at Father and Oliver who were a dozen yards away, then leaned close. "A nice young man. He seems quite infatuated with you."

"Hardly." Caroline rolled her eyes. Was her mother here to snare her a husband? Did she think that would curtail her gold seeking? "We're friends. Nothing more." Memories of his kiss swept over her, and her breath caught.

"Your expression tells me differently." She looped her arm through Caroline's. "Your eyes soften when you talk about him, and your cheeks are flushed. I think you reciprocate his feelings."

"Even if I did, nothing could ever come of it." She touched her lips. "He has plans."

"He kissed you!" Her mother frowned. "That was not part of the...he'd better declare himself to your father if he was that familiar."

Caroline froze. "Not part of what, Mother?"

"Nothing." Her mother avoided her eyes and stared at the bonnet.

Caroline yanked away her arm, and put her fists on her hips. "We're not going anywhere until you tell me what you meant."

"All right." Mother huffed out a sigh. "We've never met Oliver, but we hired him through the Pinkerton Agency to keep an eye on you."

"Mother!" Caroline stomped her foot. "How could you?"

"You were so determined to do this, and we were terrified you'd get hurt...or worse. We knew you wouldn't let us tag along, so a guard seemed the next best thing. It never occurred to us he'd fall in love with you and take liberties."

"It was one kiss, and we agreed it was a mistake."

"We—"

"I don't want to discuss this." Caroline shoved her hands into the pockets of her skirt and rushed forward. She had half a mind to jump on her horse and head to her claim where she could work until her arms ached and she was too tired to think about this mess. But she'd never let them see how much their actions hurt her. She was twenty-seven years old, and her parents still treated her like a child. Her success in the gold fields wasn't proof enough that she was capable of taking care of herself.

"I love her, sir, but I didn't mean for it to happen."

Caroline gasped. Now, what game was he playing?

Mr. Vogel lifted one eyebrow, and Oliver licked his lips, but his tongue continued to stick to the roof of his mouth. He'd felt less trepidation bringing in gang members.

"Have you told her?" The man pierced him with his gaze.

Oliver cleared his throat. Now he knew how a mouse felt under the malevolent stare of an cat. "Uh, no, sir." His voice broke, and Caroline rushed past him, skirts swirling around her legs. Where was she going in such a hurry? He cleared his throat again. "No. I've been praying about the situation and decided last night to send a telegram informing you and Mr. Pinkerton of my resignation. I've compromised the assignment by developing feelings for your daughter."

"Call me Jess."

"Sir?"

"Well, it's a bit early for Pa or Father or the like, so call me Jess."

"Early?" Oliver gulped. The man was going to think him an imbecile. "Early for what?"

"It seems like there are some kinks to work out, but if the expression on Caroline's face is any indication, at some point you're going to be my son-in-law. So we may as well drop the formalities."

"Well...uh...Jess...she's made it plain that she's not interested in marriage or me." He ran a finger around his collar. "But I'm glad you're here. I spent most of the night thinking about what to say in the telegram, but couldn't come up with the right words.

Jess snickered. "'I quit. I love Caroline' would have done the trick and wouldn't have cost you much."

"That might have brought you into town with guns blazing." Oliver shrugged, sweat pooling under his arms. "I wanted a chance to make my case."

"And what *is* your case?"

"I'm a believer now, but I've got a past I'm not proud of. I've done things. Lying. Stealing. For years." His chest tightened. May as well get his confession over with. He tugged at his hat, then poured out his heart, leaving nothing out. Finally, he fell silent.

"That's quite a story, son." Jess wrapped one arm around his shoulder. "Thanks for your honesty. Now, I'm going to tell you the truth: I know all about you from Mr. Pinkerton. We had to be sure he was sending a man of integrity to watch out for our little girl."

Oliver's jaw dropped. "You knew."

"Yep."

"And my history doesn't bother you?"

"We all have a past. Me included." He waved his hand. "But that's a story for another time. Anyway, the good news is that we don't have to be chained to our misdeeds. As believers, we've been washed clean. All that nastiness is gone."

"Yes, but I still stumble."

"As do I, but you try your best. Mr. Pinkerton says you're one of the finest men he knows." He winked. "Trouble is, we've got to convince Caroline of that fact."

"Might take some doing. Judging from her glare, she knows my association with the agency now." Oliver's stomach hollowed. "By not telling her, I've lost her trust."

"She's hurt because she has feelings. If she didn't care, she wouldn't be so upset."

"You think so?" Oliver's pulse quickened. Perhaps there was hope after all.

Chapter Twenty-One

Caroline plunked the plates on the table in front of her parents, then grabbed a third one and ladled stew onto the dish. She sat down with a huff and waited while Father said grace. A dull ache throbbed behind her left eye. She'd been fighting a headache since they'd come back from town.

Without Oliver.

When she'd returned to her parents after a lengthy argument with herself, he was absent. Her parents made some excuse about him having business to take care of, but she wasn't convinced. She'd heard his declaration of love but didn't dare stay around for the end of the conversation.

She fiddled with her bandanna. He'd intimated he cared when he encouraged her to pray and talk to Little Doe, but love? No. Not possible. Was he playing with her parents? Did he think his declaration would excuse him in her father's eyes for kissing her? A Pinkerton agent. She never saw that one coming. He could go on the stage with his acting skills.

"Honey, please don't blame Oliver. He was sworn to secrecy." Mother picked up her fork. "He's a good man, and he loves you."

"So he says." Caroline pushed a carrot chunk through the gravy. "He got bored with panning, and he's seen how much I've made. He knows you're wealthy. Perhaps marrying into the family is the easy way to prosperity." She poked the vegetable into her mouth and swallowed. Her words rang hollow. Even she didn't believe them, but she had to say something to deter her parents from insisting that she take the man as her husband. They'd been haranguing her for the last hour.

"Caroline!" Mother's eyes widened. "There's no need to insult the man."

"You're right. I'm sorry." She pierced another carrot. "I'm just out of sorts. This isn't the way it was supposed to happen." She popped the food into her mouth and chewed in silence.

From the corner of her eye, she watched her parents exchange glances. They seemed to have an entire conversation without speaking. After nearly thirty years of marriage, they could probably read each other's thoughts. She'd seen them finish each other's sentences often enough.

Mother sipped her water, then set down the cup with a muted thump. "What were your expectations? We didn't talk about them before you left."

"Simple." Caroline shrugged. "Travel here with the wagon train and work my claim until it played out or I no longer wanted to pan. I didn't expect to befriend an Indian woman or have to keep men at bay who think I don't belong. And I certainly didn't count on falling in love."

"So you do care for Oliver." Mother's forehead wrinkled. "Then why are you pushing him away?"

"Because I'm not interested in marriage. To him or anyone." Caroline laced her fingers. Better to tell them that rather a relationship would never work out whether she and Oliver loved each other or not. He would eventually realize he could find a better woman.

Her eyes filled, and she blinked away the tears hoping her parents hadn't noticed the moisture. "Not every man or woman needs to wed. I'm happy being single. Perhaps it makes me selfish, but I like not having to answer to someone. I can do what I want when I want to do it, without getting permission from some man." Her gaze slid to her father. "No offense, Father."

"None taken, but that's not the way my relationship is with your mother." He smiled at his wife. "We're partners. But she doesn't require my *permission* to do anything. Rather, she makes her decisions based on what is best for everyone. That's what you do when you're part of a family. Ultimately, I'm head of the house, but I value her input." He frowned. "I'm sorry if you view me as lording my authority over her or you."

She reached out and squeezed his hand. "That's not what I see."

"Then why are you afraid marriage will be that way with Oliver?"

Why indeed? Caroline smoothed her napkin, then sighed. "I'm not sure, because he's been kind and solicitous, never arrogant."

"Perhaps I gave you too much freedom. You may see marriage as giving that up, but it's not. I'm not sure what to say to prove that to you." Father pushed away his empty plate. "He's resigned from the assignment and has asked me for your hand."

Her eyes widened as her pulse tripped. "Resigned? What did you say?"

"I said yes, but the final answer is up to you. We won't force you into marrying him." He pinched the bridge of his nose, then sighed. "Your mother and I failed by trying to protect you. We let you do what you wished as consolation for the poor treatment you received from others, as if that would make up for hurt feelings. But only God can protect you. I know that now."

"You did what you thought was best, Father. A girl couldn't ask for better parents." She smiled at him and her mother. "Now, no more seriousness. How long do you plan to stay? Did you want to work the claim for old time's sake?"

He chuckled. "As long as you'll have us, and I'd love to do some panning." He raised his eyebrow to her mother. "Hannah?"

"Do I get to keep what I find?" She grinned at Caroline. "Because that's how it worked in my day."

Caroline giggled. "Absolutely. I wouldn't have it any other way. We'll start first thing in the morning."

A knock sounded, and Father rose and answered the door.

Oliver stood on the threshold, hat in hand. His gaze flicked from the dishes on the table to her face. "I'm sorry to interrupt your dinner. I can come back later."

"We're finished." Heart pounding, she climbed to her feet. "Do you want to join us for coffee?"

"Uh, no. I just came to tell you that I received a reply from Mr. Pinkerton. I've got another assignment if I want it." He gave her a pointed look. "If there's no reason for me to say, I'll head out as soon as I sell my claim."

Chapter Twenty-Two

The horses' hooves clomped softly on the ground as Caroline and Little Doe made their way through the woods toward the river, in the early morning light. After Oliver's stunning announcement last night, her parents had left, indicating fatigue after their journey. She knew they were giving her time alone with him.

His answers in response to her questions about his mission had been monosyllabic, and she'd given up quizzing him. He'd paced the small cabin seeming to argue with himself. She'd teased him about it, but his laughter seemed forced. Finally, when she could stand it no longer, he'd sat at the table and blurted out a marriage proposal.

She'd let him down as gently as she could, but the hurt in his eyes had been evident. Moments later, he was gone. The silence in the cabin was deafening, and she'd debated whether to run after him. But what would she say once she caught up with him? Her answer would still be no, and a long-winded explanation would only make things worse.

How long before the ache in her heart would cease?

"Hold it right there."

Caroline reined in the horse and reached toward the scabbard for her pistol. Little Doe gasped.

"Don't even think about it, or you'll be dead before you hit the ground." Willis Baldridge emerged from the trees, a revolver in each hand. "Bet you never thought you'd see me again," he said with an ugly laugh.

She pulled back her hand and frowned. "Why aren't you in jail?"

Beside her on a small pony, Little Doe stiffened.

"Because the idiot guard underestimated me." He puffed out his chest. "I escaped."

"Take me and let her go," Little Doe said. "You don't want her."

"I'm taking you both. You'll bring a good price, and then you'll be out of my hair forever." He leered at them. "I've already made the arrangements."

"But—"

"Not another word!" He waved the guns. "I've half a mind to kill you, but I need the money."

Nausea gripped Caroline, and she licked her dry lips. She exchanged a glance with Little Doe, whose eyes were wide in her ashen face.

"Don't try nothing stupid." He pointed the weapon straight at Little Doe.

"All right." Caroline raised her hands. "All right. We'll go quietly. There's no need to get violent." She frowned and gave herself a mental kick. She should have been paying attention instead of mooning over

Oliver. For the most part, the miners left her and the few other female prospectors, alone, but danger was never far in the forests and mountains. Her absentmindedness resulted in their capture by a madman. Well, she wasn't going without a fight.

"That's better." His dark eyes glinted. "Now, you *ladies* are going to get off your horses so I can tie you up. No funny stuff."

With a nod, Caroline pinned a fearful look on her face. Hopefully, this guy thought she was a sniveling female, but he'd be wrong. "You're the one with the weapon. We'll be good. I promise." She turned to Little Doe. "We wouldn't think about trying to escape and get help in town."

Little Doe's lower lip trembled, and she shook her head.

Caroline tilted her head and rolled her eyes toward the direction from which they'd come. "Go," she mouthed.

He stepped next to her horse. "Get down! I won't tell you again."

"Fine." *Please, God, don't let my skirts get tangled.* She swung her left leg over the saddle, then launched herself at the man. Her body hit him and drove them both to the ground. One arm twisted, pain shot to her shoulder. "Now, Little Doe. Go get the sheriff!"

Both weapons fell from his hands. He gripped her wrists and roared as she raked her fingers across his cheek. She fought like a wildcat, kicking and flailing. For once she was grateful for her extra height. She might not outweigh him, but she had at least five inches on the man. Could she outrun him if the chance arose?

Thundering hoofbeats faded. *Go, Little Doe. God be with her!*

His fetid breath washed over her as he tossed her off him, then jumped to his feet.

She rolled to her knees, hands searching the leaf-covered trail for one of the guns.

Shoving her to the ground with a booted foot, he bent and retrieved his weapons as she lay on the damp earth, her tangled hair over her face. Breath ragged, she scraped the strands away from her eyes and rolled over.

He stood over her, a sinister gleam in his eyes, the barrels of both revolvers pointed at her head. Blood seeped from the scratches she'd put on his cheek, and he exhaled with a huff. "You're gonna get yourself killed, missy. Them Injuns ain't gonna put up with your nonsense."

"Indians?"

"Yep, I done made an arrangement with the Pawnee to buy you." He frowned. "Had a deal for both of you, but I guess they'll have to settle for one. Now, get up. Nice and slow."

Muscles protesting, she crawled to her feet. Her pulse hammered in her veins as she pulled herself to her full height and glared at him. "You won't get away with this. They'll come for me, and you'll go to jail for a very long time."

Quick as lightning, he slapped her.

Her ears rang, and her jaw throbbed. Tears rushed to her eyes, and she blinked to dispel the moisture. Shaking, she clenched her fists and lifted her chin to glare at him.

He poked her with the muzzle. "Yer awful brave for someone on the wrong end of a gun."

"Because I know where I'm going when I die." She crossed her arms. "I'll spend eternity with God. Can you say the same?"

Uncertainty darkened his eyes, then he barked a harsh laugh. "Good one. There ain't no life after this one. You gotta take what you can, then you die. That's it."

Peace flooded her, and she nearly giggled. *Really, Lord. You've arranged for me to tell this man about You and Your Son? Here goes nothing.* She cleared her throat. "Have you ever read the Bible, Mr. Baldridge?"

"Just a bunch of fairy tales."

"No, the Bible was written by men who knew God personally. Others spent time with His Son, Jesus, while He was on earth. He's the One who created us, and He wants us to live with Him forever. If we believe in Him, we can do that."

"Even if what you say is true, He don't want someone like me." He looked mulish. "It's too late."

"It's never too late."

The gun wavered, then he straightened and tightened his grip on the weapon. He pulled a rope from his saddlebag. "Enough of yer yammering. Daylight's burning, and I gotta hide out somewhere until the heat is off." With quick motions, he grabbed her wrists with one calloused palm, then holstered the revolver, and bound her hands together. He tied the end of the line over the pommel on his horse's saddle. He hurried to Spirit and smacked the mare's rump. "Git!"

The horse turned her head and eyed Caroline as if she knew better than to listen to the bandit.

"I said, git!" Willis shoved the horse who reared, then galloped down the trail.

Caroline swallowed. *Keep me safe, Father. I'd like to see my parents again. And Oliver.*

Chapter Twenty-Three

"Mr. Llewellyn! Mr. Llewellyn!"

Oliver's head whipped around.

Flushed and breathing heavily, Little Doe clung to her horse as she brought the animal to a stop. She slid from the saddle and crumpled to the ground. Tears streamed down her cheeks.

A chill swept over him, and he squatted next to the young woman. "What's wrong? Where's Caroline?"

She gripped his arms. "Willis. He took her. He tried to take us both, but Caroline....she fight him...I got away."

"Baldridge?" Oliver's heart pounded in his ears. "He's out of jail?"

"He escaped."

"How? Never mind, it's not important." He pulled out his handkerchief and pressed it into one of Little Doe's hands. "Tell me everything."

Mopping her eyes, she took a shuddering breath and recounted all that had happened, then said, "I should have stayed. He is angry. I'm afraid he'll kill her."

"It's good you didn't remain, otherwise, I wouldn't know about the situation." *Please, God, keep Caroline safe.* "We'll find her. Are you able to stand?"

Little Doe nodded, and he helped her to her feet.

His gaze swept over the tent village where the prospectors were beginning to stir. Most tried to be at their claims just after sunup, but it seemed that many had gotten a late start today. *A gift from You, Lord?* "I'll make a posse from these guys. Can you and Ned head to town and inform Sheriff Pickett?"

"Yes, but the sheriff won't like that you are going without him."

"I need to get a head start. Every minute we wait, the trail grows colder." He shrugged. "Tell him I'll leave a path a mile wide. He won't be able to miss it. He'll need to notify Caroline's parents, too."

"Okay." She squeezed his forearm, then stepped back, and gave him a tremulous smile. "Be careful. I will pray."

"Thanks. We'll need it." Mind racing, he double-checked Ranger's tack. It was tempting to leap on the horse and tear into the woods, but he'd be no good to anyone if he fell off the animal because he hadn't properly secured every leather strap.

From the corner of his eye, he saw Little Doe wend her way through the tents to find Ned. Good. One thing taken care of. Finished with the horse, he put two fingers to his mouth and whistled, blowing three long blasts followed by three short ones. Around the camp, men turned toward him. He raised his arms and shouted, "Miss Vogel has been abducted, and I need help finding her." The miners wandered toward him, and he continued, "Some of you have had your differences with her, but now is the time to set those aside, so we can bring her back alive." His voice broke, and he cleared his throat. "The man who took her has a history of hurting women, so we need to find her...fast. Who's with me?"

Prospectors crowded forward, raising their hands.

His heart swelled. *Thank You, God.* "All right. There can't be too many of us, or he'll hear us coming." He pointed to ten of the men. "I'll take you fellas. The rest of you can go about your business, and I wish you a successful day. And if any of you are men of faith, I'd appreciate your prayers."

As the miners who weren't selected wandered off, he addressed the remaining men. "Mount up as quick as you can. We leave in fifteen minutes. Sooner if everyone is ready."

They trotted away, and he hurried into his tent to collect his belongings, already packed in preparation for leaving. He slung his bulging saddlebags across Ranger's back, then attached his bedroll. He went into the tent to check if he'd left anything of value. His gaze surveyed the small enclosure. Empty except for the cot and crate he'd used for a nightstand, items that would convey to the man he'd sold them to. The most recent arrival in a long line of fortune hunters.

After a final glance around the space, he strode outside. All ten men sat on the horses, faces set in determination. A swarthy man with a heavy beard put two fingers to the brim of his hat. "All present and accounted for, sir. Waiting for your orders."

"Done some military time?"

"Yes, sir. Fought the Mexicans back in forty-eight."

"Yeah, me, too." He climbed onto the horse. "Little Doe is heading for the sheriff, and hopefully he'll be on our heels. The plan is to track Caroline, then wait for the law. We're not judge, jury, or executioner unless she's in trouble or he spots us and starts shooting. Then anything goes, but only if you've got clear sight. Her safety is paramount. Got that?"

The group nodded, and he sent another prayer heavenward. He patted Ranger's neck, then kneed the horse into a trot. Minutes later, he caught sight of Caroline's riderless mare cantering in his direction. "Whoa," he hollered, and the animal drew up short with a snort.

Oliver slid from Ranger and approached Spirit. The mare shied but didn't bolt. He held out a hand, palm down. "Easy, girl. You remember me." The animal nickered softly. "That's right. It's me. You okay?" He stroked her muzzle, then ran his hands over her to check for injuries. She was fine, and he blew out a deep breath. Gesturing to the closest man, he said, "She's with you."

"Yes, sir." The man walked his horse to Spirit and took the reins.

"All right. Let's go." Oliver mounted Ranger, and they continued through the path in the woods, his gaze seeking the smallest clue. A well-used trail, branches on either side were broken, and hoofprints cluttered the ground, but he hadn't been considered the best scout in his division for nothing. He would find her.

Minutes later, they arrived at the scene of the incident. From the scuff marks and disturbed leaves, he visualized what happened and grimaced. Caroline had put up a fight. But she'd lost, and the man had taken her. How badly was she hurt? His stomach clenched. She had to be frightened. *Hold on! I'm coming.*

He studied the ground. A set of hoofprints veered into the trees with boot prints behind. Too small to be a man's. His pulse quickened. For some reason he hadn't put her on the horse with him. At least, she wasn't pressed up against the man with his filthy arms around her. And making her walk would slow them down.

Oliver looked at the sky. If he calculated correctly, it'd been nearly two hours since her nightmare began. Worst case, they were six to eight miles ahead, but probably less. Still plenty of daylight. He turned the stallion toward the woods and clucked his tongue. They progressed about a mile when he spied a scrap of white fabric. Her handkerchief! Good girl!

He jumped down, grabbed the hanky, and stuffed it into his pocket before getting back on the horse. They traversed another mile or so when he found another tiny bit of material and more boot prints. She'd managed to tear off part of her sleeve, and he picked up that, too.

They continued on, the man's trail as easy to follow as if it'd been whitewashed. Either he was arrogant enough to think he couldn't be followed, or he didn't have a clue about how to mask his path. Either reason worked for Oliver.

Another mile passed. Then another.

In the distance, Oliver heard voices. He fisted his hand and held up his arm to halt the posse. He dismounted, then gestured for them to do the same. They crowded around him, eyes riveted on his face. He leaned toward them and whispered, "You all wait here. I'm going to creep up on them, get the lay of the land. I'll be back with a plan."

One of the men cocked his head. "Ain't we waitin' for the sheriff?"

"Maybe. I'll let you know what I find."

Oliver crouched and crept forward. He darted from tree to tree, remaining hidden as he approached Caroline and her abductor. Oliver stopped about thirty yards from them. They were in a clearing, and the man had the horse's left front leg pulled between his knees as he inspected the animal's hoof. A two-gun holster hung on his hips, Colt revolvers if Oliver wasn't mistaken.

Dirty and disheveled, Caroline stood at the end of a rope that was attached to the saddle. Her shoulders sagged, and dark smudges hung beneath her eyes. Her hair had come unpinned and hung down her back in a riot of curls. The bandanna was gone, and the angry, puckered skin of her scars contrasted to her wan cheeks.

He pursed his lips and imitated a mourning dove.

Caroline's head shot up, and she straightened her spine. She swiveled her neck and seemed to search the area. Her captor continued to work on the horse's hoof.

Oliver repeated the call, waited a handful of seconds, then called again.

A smile tugged at her lips, then she schooled her features and shot a look at the man.

Yes! She knew he was here. How she knew was beyond him, but perhaps God had put the thought in her head. Or perhaps his bird imitations needed work, and she realized the noise had come from a human being.

The man would only be distracted for a few moments longer. The opportunity for rescue was now. Oliver took a deep breath, then edged back the way he'd come until he was another twenty yards away. On the balls of his feet, he made his way halfway around the clearing, then crept toward it. Fortunately, the man was keeping up a running dialogue of complaints about the stone lodged in the horse's shoe.

Gun in hand, Oliver sneaked closer to the glade inch by inch. He stopped behind the final tree that stood a yard between him and the man. He peeked around the trunk, and Caroline's eyes widened. He shook his head. She froze.

"Finally." Willis dropped the horse's leg and stepped back.

Oliver hurled himself toward the man and brought the butt of his pistol down on his head. Willis's knees buckled, and he collapsed with a grunt as he hit the ground. His eyes rolled up into his head, and he stilled. In a flash, Oliver removed the man's guns from the holster, rushed to Caroline, and unbound her wrists. "Hold those on him while I bind him."

She nodded, her lips trembling.

He made quick work of trussing up the man as the posse appeared among the trees.

Staring into her crystal-green eyes, he gulped. What had he been thinking when he decided to leave? He'd convince her of his love if it was the last thing he did.

Chapter Twenty-Four

The following day, Caroline stood in the middle of her cabin and shoved the last of her goods into the saddlebag. Mother sat on the cot, and Father paced.

Caroline huffed out a sigh. "Look, I appreciate you coming out to see me, and I wish I could stay, but I need to move on. Get a fresh start."

Mother grabbed her arm. "That's what you said when you left Georgia. How many fresh starts do you need before you realize you've got to stop running?"

"I'm not running." Caroline shook off her mother's hand. "I'm done panning for gold. I've earned enough to live comfortably for a while...until I decide what I want to do next."

Father raked his hands through his hair.

She shoved her hands into her pockets. "I'll be fine. Willis is dead. He tried to escape the posse, and one of the men shot him. There's no need to worry about me."

He gave her a quick hug, then stepped back. "As your parents, we'll always worry about you." He grinned. "Even when you're sixty and we're eighty. It's what parents do."

"Fair enough." Caroline chuckled. "When do you head home?"

"We're not in a hurry to return, so we've decided to do a little sightseeing. Visit some of the places we've heard about." He winked at her mother. "Make it a second honeymoon."

Mother giggled. "I can't wait."

Caroline's face warmed. Seeing her parents act like two young lovers was embarrassing. And bittersweet. Last night, after reaching the cabin, Oliver had proposed. She'd turned him down. Again. But he hadn't seemed hurt this time. He was...resolute. As if he'd come to a decision. He bade her good night and left the tiny abode. Sleep had been a long time coming for her.

She buckled the leather satchel and straightened her spine. She might love him, but she couldn't trust him with her heart. He'd lied to her. No. It had been more than lying. He'd pretended to be someone he wasn't. He'd hidden his true identity from her. She couldn't live with a man who practiced that kind of subterfuge.

"I'm off. The wagon train won't wait." She smiled at her folks. "I'll write when I'm able." She lifted an eyebrow. "You haven't stowed another Pinkerton agent in this group, have you?"

Father's lips twisted. "Funny. You know we only did what we thought was right."

"Yes, which makes me wonder if you're still doing it."

He tucked a stray hair behind her ear. "A fair question, but no, we're not. You've got a good head on your shoulders, and we'll pray God keeps you safe. Can you forgive an old man for his faults?"

She drew him into a tight embrace, tears threatening. "Always."

Sniffling, Mother rose and wrapped her arms around the two of them. "We love you, honey. Take care of yourself."

Caroline nodded and extricated herself from their grasp. She swallowed against the lump in her throat, picked up her bag, and slung it over her shoulder. Her trunk was stowed in the wagon she was sharing with a family. With a last look, she headed out the door.

Booted feet clomping against the hard ground, she hurried toward Spirit before she could change her mind and return to the fold of her family. She climbed onto the mare and urged her forward. When they cleared the tent village, Caroline kneed the animal into a gallop. The sooner she put Pike's Peak behind her, the better.

Oliver hummed to himself as sauntered toward the tent village. The midmorning sun warmed his back, and the day promised to be another scorcher. Hopefully, Caroline was still asleep. She'd had a harrowing experience, although she'd come through like a trooper. Not once breaking down into tears, she'd ridden Spirit from the clearing, surrounded by him and half the posse. The other half took her captor to town. Unfortunately, the man had tried to escape and been killed during the scuffle.

Thank You for how things worked out, Lord. I'm sorry the man is dead. But You kept Caroline safe, and none of the posse was injured during the process.

He patted Ranger's neck. "She'll be surprised to see us, old boy. After turning me down last night, she probably thinks I'm still leaving, but I'm going to stay and be her friend. Show her she can trust me. That I'm a man of my word." He sighed. "It might take months, but I'm going to get her to love me."

The horse whinnied, and Oliver laughed. "You're telling me to be patient, aren't you?"

He approached the village and wended his way through the tents until he got to the cabin. He slid from the horse and sprinted to the door. Taking off his hat, he smoothed his unruly hair. He squared his shoulders, then raised his hand and knocked.

Silence.

Another knock. "Caroline? It's me. Oliver."

Not a sound.

"Caroline?" He pressed the latch, and the door swung open. The tiny room was vacant. The cot stripped of its bedding, the crate by the bed empty of her personal effects. Her trunk was missing. She was gone. Left without a trace. Had she decided to return home with her parents? She claimed that was the last thing she'd planned to do, but that decision had been made before her abduction.

Even better. Her folks seemed to like him. He could move to Georgia, proving how much he cared for her. Woo her with their help.

He exited the cabin and jumped on the horse. "Looks like it's back to town, Ranger." Once out from among the tents, he clicked his teeth. "Hyah." The horse shot forward, and they raced toward Boulder City. Arriving at the bustling streets, he steered Ranger to the hotel, slid from the saddle, and tied the stallion to the post. Oliver yanked open the door and rushed inside. Looking neither left nor right, he hurried to the front desk. "I'm—"

"Oliver?"

He whirled.

Caroline's parents walked toward him. Her mother's forehead was creased into a deep frown. "You're looking for her."

"Yes." He grabbed his hat from his head. "I don't know if she told you that I proposed last night. She turned me down, but I aim to wear her down until she says yes. Gently, but persistently." He searched their faces. "I hope I have your blessing. Is she upstairs?"

Her father shook his head. "I'm afraid not, son. She left on a wagon train headed south to Texas. She wants to try homesteading. Cattle ranching is big down there."

"And you let her go?" His face warmed. "I'm sorry, sir. That was uncalled for."

"No apology necessary." He smiled. "But if you aim to catch her, you'd better get moving. She's had a five-hour head start."

"Don't you worry. Those trains can't do more than twenty miles in a day, fewer in this mountainous area."

Her mother kissed his cheek. "God be with you."

"Thank you, ma'am...sir." He clamped on his hat and raced out the door. He wrenched the traces from the post and leapt onto Ranger's back. He wheeled the horse around and slapped the reins, and leaned over the animal's neck. "Ride like the wind."

Ranger surged forward, his legs eating up the distance to the edge of town. Three miles outside the community, he caught up with the wagons. A cloud of dust followed the unwieldy conveyances, and he waved his hand to clear the air in front of his face. He squinted through the particles and slowed the horse to a walk. As he passed the pedestrians, he checked each face.

Then he saw her statuesque bloomer-clad form.

Leading Spirit by the halter, she ambled alongside one of the wagons.

His heart skittered, and he pressed one hand to his chest. "Buck up, man. You've faced dangerous killers." He urged the stallion forward, and seconds later, he drew up behind her and slipped from the saddle. "Caroline?"

Her head whipped toward him, and her emerald eyes lit up. She threw herself into his arms. "You came," her voice wavered. "You hunted me down, and you came. I didn't think you would do that."

His arms tightened around her, his face inches from hers. "I would have searched to the ends of the earth to find you. I love you, Caroline. And I'd like take the rest of my life to show you just how much. Will you marry me?" So much for wooing her gently.

"I love you, too. I kept fighting the feeling, but I can't deny it any longer." She beamed at him. "Yes, I'll marry you."

He bent his head and brushed his lips against hers, then pulled back and grinned. "Then it looks like I'm headed to Texas."

"You're coming with me?"

"Absolutely. I don't care where I live, as long as it's with you."

Three months later

Epilogue

Caroline's stomach buzzed as if a swarm of hummingbirds had taken flight. Palms moist, she stepped out of the carriage, then tugged at the bodice of her teal gown. The sizzling Texas sun glinted off the windows of the house. Her house. She took a deep breath and studied the simple structure where Oliver waited inside.

Constructed in only three weeks, the single-story farmhouse-style building featured a wide porch that wrapped around three sides. Her face warmed. She'd worked with one of San Antonio's foremost architects to design the place, but Oliver had thrown in his two cents and insisted on five bedrooms, saying with a wicked grin that more might be required later. The parlor, dining room, kitchen, and office were large with lots of windows, but he'd ordered the newfangled spring roller window shades that could be closed to keep out the heat. Best of all, she'd splurged and installed an indoor privy.

The journey to San Antonio had taken nearly two months. Sixty days of difficult, exhausting travel made sweet by Oliver's presence. He'd checked in with the trail boss who'd agreed to let him join the train because of his experience on the trip to Pike's Peak as well as his background as a Pinkerton. He was again second-in-command and ensured that everyone did their bit to support the group and themselves. He arranged hunting parties when the need for fresh meat arose and created a schedule for guard duty to ensure the travelers weren't caught unawares by Indian raids. Aware of keeping propriety, he slept under the stars hundreds of yards from wherever her wagon stopped for the night.

Over the course of the trip, they'd grown closer to each other and the Lord as they read the Bible and prayed together when Oliver's schedule allowed. His gentle but forthright manner earned him the respect of the entire wagon train, and the women had drawn her into their circle, becoming dear friends with each passing day, although she still missed Little Doe who had accepted Ned's marriage proposal and remained in Boulder City.

After the ladies discovered she and Oliver were getting married, they'd thrown themselves into planning and preparation with abandon. She'd tried to stem the tide of activity, but her attempts were futile, and she'd finally given up. The night before the wagon train was to arrive in San Antonio, the entire group gave them a pounding. Typically done for the new minister of a church during which congregants bring the man and his family a pound of flour, coffee, or other necessities, the ladies had declared the party a bridal pounding.

And now the entire group was gathered in the living room to witness her marriage. Her parents had sent a congratulatory telegram indicating they would visit after the turn of the year once the newlyweds were settled.

"Are you ready, Miss Vogel?" Micah stood, hat in hand, wearing a freshly pressed cotton shirt, and jeans, his hair slicked down.

She nodded and gave the trail boss a watery smile, pressing her hand against her middle to stem the fluttering. "Absolutely. Just taking in the moment."

"As well you should. Times like this are precious and too often rushed through." He crooked his arm. "You're pretty as a picture, and I'm proud to escort you."

Tucking one hand inside his elbow, she lifted her skirts and ascended the stairs. Another deep breath, and she stepped across the threshold. She gasped at the riot of blooms that transformed the living room into a veritable garden, but she only had eyes for the towering, handsome man with ebony hair in the front of the room.

Faces of her guests blurred as she glided across the polished black cherrywood floor toward her groom. Toward her future. His gaze was bright as if lit from within, and his teeth flashed white against his tanned skin. She reached his side, and he took her hands in his, then bent to place a kiss on her lips.

"Hey, let's not get ahead of ourselves." The preacher of the local church chuckled and poked Oliver.

"Sorry, Pastor." He winked at her and squeezed her fingers, not looking the least bit apologetic. "I got caught up in the moment."

She giggled, her lips tingling. She'd run from his love, but he'd tracked her down, and now they would travel together for a lifetime.

THE END

What did you think of *Gold Rush Bride: Caroline?*

Thank you so much for purchasing *Gold Rush Bride: Caroline.* You could have selected any number of books to read, but you chose this book.

I hope it added encouragement and exhortation to your life. If so, it would be nice if you could share this book with your family and friends by posting to Facebook (www.facebook.com) and/or Twitter (www.twitter.com).

If you enjoyed this book and found some benefit in reading it, I'd appreciate it if you could take some time to post a review on Amazon, Goodreads, Kobo, Bookbub, GooglePlay, Apple Books, or other book review site of your choice. Your feedback and support will help me to improve my writing craft for future projects and make this book even better.
Thank you again for your purchase.

Blessings,
Linda Shenton Matchett

Want to see where it all began? Read on for the first chapter of *Gold Rush Bride Hannah*, book 1 in the *Gold Rush Brides* series.

March 1829

Dahlonega, GA

Chapter One

Reverberations from the gunshot echoed among the hills surrounding Hannah Lauman's property as she gripped the rifle and watched the cougar disappear through the trees. Winter had apparently not been kind to the gaunt and shaggy animal, prompting its boldness to approach the homestead. Fortunately, Quinn had taught her to shoot, so she could protect herself during the times he was away from their claim. Four-legged beasts weren't the only predators she'd had to scare off after word got out about how much gold she and her husband were pulling from Yahoola Creek.

Despite a chilly gust that tugged at her skirt, perspiration trickled down her spine and pooled under arms. No matter how often she used a gun, she'd never get used to the thunderous boom or the weapon's kick against her shoulder. She'd sport a bruise by nightfall. She reloaded the rifle, then leaned the gun against the clothes-line post next to the basket filled with wet laundry. She needed to be ready if the big cat decided to return. Would she ever get used to living so remotely?

Hannah wiped the sweat off her forehead with her sleeve, then blew out a deep breath. Philosophizing over her lot in life wouldn't get the chores done, and she had plenty to complete before Quinn's return by dinner, provided he wasn't late. Some women had to worry about their husbands' penchants for drinking, gambling, and other detrimental pursuits, but Quinn's worst habit was getting caught up in the beauty of the outdoors and losing track of time.

Panning this week had been more productive than usual and storing the accumulated flakes and nuggets in the cabin was never a good idea, so today's journey to Gainesville was his third trip to the bank. How long the gold would hold out was anyone's guess, so she should probably be down at the water's edge, but the two of them were out of clean clothes, and she hadn't swept or dusted in days. She wasn't so gold-hungry that she'd live in a pigsty.

She grabbed one of Quinn's shirts and hung the cotton garment over the line, then bent and picked up another. She ought to warn the other miners about the wildcat, but perhaps the gunshot would bring one of the neighbors running so she wouldn't have to seek them out. She continued to hang the laundry, periodically glancing over her shoulder in case the cougar decided to return. Known for their humanlike screams, the tawny cats crept with silent stealth when on the prowl.

Finished with the clothes, she gave one last look toward the forest, then picked up the basket and headed toward the cabin. Inside, she lit one of the lamps to push away the gloom from the small abode. She'd put her foot down when Quinn suggested they build a soddy, but some days the tiny two-room abode didn't seem much better. With only one small window next to the door, the interior remained dim except on the sunniest of days.

"Hello, the house!" A shrill voice sounded in the yard.

Hannah stepped to the doorway and waved.

Glenda Thompson, the wife of another miner a few claims away waddled toward her, the woman's swollen stomach evidence of her late-term pregnancy. She carried a towel-wrapped bundle. "Good afternoon, Hannah. I made several loaves of bread and thought y'all might be able to use one."

"Real bread sounds heavenly. We've been eating biscuits with most of our meals. Quinn will be thrilled."

The petite blonde woman handed her the loaf, then rested her arms on her belly. "Where is that husband of yours? I didn't see him on my way over. Thought he'd be down at the water with the rest of the boys sifting through the sand."

"He went into Gainesville. Should be back any time."

"Another trip to the bank?" Glenda's eyebrow lifted. "Y'all must be doin' better than the rumors say."

Hannah shrugged. "Quinn's no Stephen Girard. We won't be financing the government any time soon."

Glenda giggled, then sighed. "At least you're gettin' by."

"Not quite the thrills and riches we were promised, huh?" Hannah tucked a stray hair behind her ear. "We've done better than some, but the work is backbreaking, and the worry about claim jumpers, injury, and wildlife is wearing." She snapped her fingers. "By the way, a cougar wandered into the yard a short time ago. You might have heard the gunshot."

"I thought Quinn might be huntin' squirrels or rabbits. That's bad news about the wildcat. I'll be sure to pass the word." Glenda huffed out a breath. "You ever wonder what life would be like if you weren't diggin' for gold day in and day out?"

"More often than you'd think." She gestured to the garments flapping on the line. "If you'd have been here earlier, you'd have heard me arguing with myself. Like I said, we're doing all right, but I miss the conveniences we had in Atlanta as well as the socializing. It gets lonely." Especially with no children, but Hannah wouldn't get into that. Married for nearly ten years, she'd yet to conceive. And the longer her childlessness went on, the farther apart she and Quinn grew. She shook her head to clear the morose thoughts. "Everything okay?"

"We've about played out our claim. Might be movin' on." Glenda's chin trembled. "There are a few claims available upriver, so Bart's thinkin' of buying one of those. This was going to be our chance to get ahead. Scrimpin' by on a blacksmith's income before comin' here was better than this. I'm not sure how much more gold chasin' I can do, but Bart doesn't listen to me. He's sure we're gonna strike it big."

"He might not be wrong. Quite a few claims have produced significantly." Hannah rocked on her heels. "We only found dribs and drabs when we first arrived. We kept at it, and finally hit a good vein."

"Yeah, but we're gonna have a family to think about soon. We need a stable salary." Glenda rubbed at the cross dangling from a long silver chain around her neck. "I've been prayin' Bart will come to his senses, but nothin' yet."

"I'm sorry things are hard for you." Hannah fiddled with the edge of the towel. If their claim hadn't produced, would Quinn have been willing to walk away? Go back to their staid life in the city? If truth be told, they'd done better working the gold. A bit of a dreamer, he'd held and lost numerous jobs over the course of their lives together, always moving on to opportunities that were supposed to be bigger and better. The day he'd come home and announced he'd purchased a gold claim from a widow, they'd argued well into the night. Then she'd decided that working together might sweeten their marriage, draw them close again. She was still waiting for that to happen. What was it with men and their desire for fortune and glory?

Thundering hooves pounded, and Hannah's head whipped toward the sound. Chet Fawley, Dahlonega's sheriff crouched low over his horse's neck. He brought the animal to a halt, then slid from the saddle. His face with lined with fatigue and sadness.

Hannah's stomach hollowed, and her hand flew to her throat. There was no doubt the man brought bad news. "Quinn?" Her lips moved, but no sound came out.

Sheriff Fawley removed his dusty Stetson and licked his lips. "I'm sorry, Miz Lauman. Your husband's dead. Ambushed outside of town."

Dizziness struck, and she swayed. Glenda wrapped her arm around Hannah's shoulder, keeping her from falling to the ground in a heap. Dots of light danced in her vision, and roaring, like an approaching train, filled her ears. A lump formed in her throat. "Ambushed?" Her voice caught, and she swallowed. "Who would want to murder my husband?"

"Looks like the work of the Cherokees. I've got my boys looking into things as we speak." He ducked his head. "I guess you'll be pulling out and going back to Atlanta, so be sure to let me know how I can contact you when I solve the case. Shouldn't be long."

Overhead, the sun broke out from behind a bank of clouds casting a bright beam onto Hannah's face. A slight breeze brushed her cheeks as if God had reached down to remind her of His love and presence, even during this terrible turn of events. Hannah squared her shoulders. "I'm not going anywhere, Sheriff. I've got a claim to work."

Acknowledgments

Although writing a book is a solitary task, it is not a solitary journey. There have been many who have helped and encouraged me along the way.

My parents, Richard and Jean Shenton, who presented me with my first writing tablet and encouraged me to capture my imagination with words. Thanks, Mom and Dad!

Scribes212 – my ACFW online critique group: Valerie Goree, Marcia Lahti, and the late Loretta Boyett (passed on to Glory, but never forgotten). Without your input, my writing would not be nearly as effective.

Eva Marie Everson – my mentor/instructor with Christian Writers' Guild. You took a timid, untrained student and turned her into a writer. Many thanks!

SincNE, and the folks who coordinate the Crimebake Writing Conference. I have attended many writing conferences, but without a doubt, Crimebake is one of the best. The workshops, seminars, panels, critiques, and every tiny aspect are well-executed, professional, and educational.

Special thanks to Hank Phillippi Ryan, Halle Ephron, and Roberta Isleib for your encouragement and spot-on critiques of my work.

Thanks to my Book Brigade who provide information, encouragement, and support.

A special shout out to reader Dawn LeGros who suggested the name Spirit for Caroline's horse.

Paula Proofreader (https://paulaproofreader.wixsite.com/home): I'm so glad I found you! My work is cleaner because of your eagle eye. Any mistakes are completely mine.

A heartfelt thank you to my brothers, Jack Shenton and Douglas Shenton, and my sister, Susan Shenton Greger for being enthusiastic cheerleaders during my writing journey. Your support means more than you'll know.

My husband, Wes, deserves special kudos for understanding my need to write. Thank you for creating my writing room – it's perfect, and I'm thankful for it every day. Thank you for your willingness to accept a house that's a bit cluttered, laundry that's not always done, and meals on the go. I love you.

And finally, to God be the glory. I thank Him for giving me the gift of writing and the inspiration to tell stories that shine the light on His goodness and mercy.

Other Titles
Romance

Love's Harvest, Wartime Brides, Book 1

Love's Rescue, Wartime Brides, Book 2

Love's Belief, Wartime Brides, Book 3

Love's Allegiance, Wartime Brides, Book 4

Love Found in Sherwood Forest

A Love Not Forgotten

On the Rails

A Doctor in the House

Spies & Sweethearts, Sisters in Service, Book 1

The Mechanic & the MD, Sisters in Service, Book 2

The Widow & the War Correspondent, Sisters in Service, Book 3

Love at First Flight

Multi-author Series

A Bride for Seamus (Proxy Brides, 48)

A Bride for Seamus (Proxy Brides, 62)

Dinah's Dilemma (Westward Home and Hearts Mail-Order Brides, 10)

Rayne's Redemption (Westward Home and Hearts Mail-Order Brides, 15)

Legacy of Love (Keepers of the Light, 10)

Vanessa's Replacement Valentine, (Brides of Pelican Rapids, 13)

Mystery
Under Fire, Ruth Brown Mystery Series, Book 1

Gold Rush Bride Caroline

Under Ground, Ruth Brown Mystery Series, Book 2

Under Cover, Ruth Brown Mystery Series, Book 3

Murder of Convenience, Women of Courage, Book 1

Murder at Madison Square Garden, Women of Courage, Book 2

Non-Fiction
WWII Word Find, Volume 1

Biography

Linda Shenton Matchett writes about ordinary people who did extraordinary things in days gone by. She is a volunteer docent and archivist at the Wright Museum of WWII. Born in Baltimore, Maryland, a stone's throw from Fort McHenry, she has lived in historical places most of her life. Now located in central New Hampshire, Linda's favorite activities include exploring historical sites and immersing herself in the imaginary worlds created by other authors.

Website/blog: http://www.LindaShentonMatchett.com
Newsletter signup (receive a free short story):
https://mailchi.mp/74bb7b34c9c2/lindashentonmatchettnewsletter
Facebook: http://www.facebook.com/LindaShentonMatchettAuthor
Pinterest: http://www.pinterest.com/lindasmatchett
Amazon: https://www.amazon.com/Linda-Shenton-Matchett/e/B01DNB54S0
Goodreads: http://www.goodreads.com/author_linda_matchett
Bookbub: http://www.bookbub.com/authors/linda-shenton-matchett